"In *Crystelle Mourning* not only are we given the gift of an inspiring main character and her journey forward and back, but also the pleasure of experiencing a first-time novelist, with so much promise, burst upon the scene."

—Kevin Powell

"Lovely and earth scorching."

—Tayari Jones, Hurston/Wright Legacy Award winner

Crystelle Mourning

A NOVEL

Eisa Nefertari Ulen

WASHINGTON SQUARE PRESS

New York London Toronto Sydney

Washington Square Press
A Division of Simon & Schuster, Inc.
1230 Avenue of the Americas
New York, NY 10020

This book is a work of fiction. Names, characters, places, and
incidents either are products of the author's imagination or are used
fictitiously. Any resemblance to actual events or locales or persons,
living or dead, is entirely coincidental.

Copyright © 2006 by Eisa Ulen

All rights reserved, including the right to reproduce
this book or portions thereof in any form whatsoever.
For information address Atria Books Subsidiary Rights Department,
1230 Avenue of the Americas, New York, NY 10020

First Washington Square Press trade paperback edition September 2007

WASHINGTON SQUARE PRESS and colophon are registered trademarks of
Simon & Schuster, Inc.

For information about special discounts for bulk purchases,
please contact Simon & Schuster Special Sales at 1-800-456-6798
or business@simonandschuster.com

Manufactured in the United States of America

1 3 5 7 9 10 8 6 4 2

ISBN-13: 978-0-7432-7758-7
ISBN-10:   0-7432-7758-9
ISBN-13: 978-0-7432-7759-4 (pbk)
ISBN-10:   0-7432-7759-7 (pbk)

For Diane Maria City
Forever

Lights flash against black going everywhere. The tangle is hair twisted, falling upward against a rush. Displaced air twisting tangles falling upward. Lips wave and roll like tiny seas. Salt water filled by eyes open wide. Air rippling against lips in the rush, in the fall. Eyes the fall. Shut one and eye the fall. I the fall. Ears ringing . . .

Prologue

The rhythm was deep and long and, when you stood still, you could feel the beat reverberate, pulse through your blood-line, knock along your soul. You smiled. Out across the crowd—enough folk to fill a basement to overflowing—you could see all the faces that mattered. People you'd known since before you could remember. People who had just always been around.

You stood on the steps, looking out over bodies hot and wet and strong in the dance. Heat hung, suspended, like a spirit with its descendants, a spirit that had not yet aligned with the ancestors. Heat hung so thick, you could ingest it, taste the funk of youth, feel it roll down your throat, coat your stomach, pump to your heart, spread to your toes.

"They need to open the windows down here," Tara yelled over the music.

"They are open," Shelley pointed to the wall. "What they need to do is turn on that old air conditioner over there."

"It's hot," Michelle said.

You raised your hand to touch her hair, pressed down hard on the feathered bangs in front and the flip in the back.

All four of you girls, you almost women, walked down the brown, wood steps. You saw bodies beneath your feet. The tops of heads of boys, almost men, clustered in a corner under the stairs. Their heads were nodding to the beat, just like your heart, just like your lungs surrounding your heart. Even your bones, the rib cage holding all your essential organs, vibrated with song.

You clustered, too. All four of you gathered along that old credenza. You leaned against the imitation wood behind you, hands turned backward so the fleshy part of your palms pressed against the front edge and your fingers curled along the top toward the basement walls. Your elbows angled behind you.

All four of you wore red straight-leg pants and full blouses, your wide belts cinched just enough at the waist to flare your shirts around your hips. You wore tiny heels, black pumps, and felt grown.

You looked for him, thought you spotted him standing by the sofa up against the far wall. You smiled, then realized that wasn't him, and looked away.

Everything happened after that.

Boys slipped over to your crew. One by one they pulled all your girls out into the mass of indistinguishable bodies shifting like shadows in the darkness. You stood alone. Watching couples on the edge of the crowd, people on the periphery, you saw them tilt and sway, moving their shoulders, turning. Girls danced back a step, turned around, threw their arms out in front of them. Boys stepped up behind, moved closer to them, touching, not touching, sometimes grinding. People soul clapped through the funk.

Then you saw him. Knew it was him even before you could see his features clearly. He smiled and cocked his head to the side, threw his body into a mock gangster lean to step-dance up to where you stood. He did this from across the room. One hand held his chin, like he was sizing you up for the first time, and he swung the other arm back and forth with each long-legged strut. He strolled. You looked down and laughed and looked up again to see that other girl. A dancing girl. The dancing girl turned around and looked at you, dead in the eye. She smirked. *An I got him now.*

You saw him stop leaning, stop smiling, and you smirked back as he sidestepped that dancing girl and tried to walk through the crowd, walk regularly, to you. He walked around dancing couples, and you thought he looked like a video game icon trying to maneuver obstacles, trying to get bonus points. You laughed and smiled. You watched as he faded into darkness, stepped into light, faded. You stopped laughing. Stopped smiling too.

Manny jumped in. Out of nowhere.

"What's up?"

"The ceiling, the sky, the price of rice." You rolled your eyes.

Manny grinned without showing his teeth. His full lips stretched tight, puckered, then stretched again. He looked over at his boys by the couch, nodded his head. "Stop playing, girl."

"Stop playing what, Manny?" You looked around his shoulder, tried to see into the dark. "Whatchu want?"

"Girl, stop playing. I saw you checkin' me out earlier." You leaned up, off the credenza. Took a step to the right to try to see. He turned, shifted to his left so he could still face you. "Come on, let's dance."

"Naw, it ain't that kinda party."

"What you talkin' 'bout? It is a party."

Then you looked in his face. "Not over here it ain't."

Manny was not looking at you. He was glancing at his boys again. Then he put his hand out to lead you into the crowd.

"You didn't hear me?" You looked at his hand, rolled your eyes up to meet his gaze, and folded your arms.

"Why you tryin' to play me?"

"Ain't nobody tryin' to play you, boy. You know I got a man. Why you all in my face?"

"I saw you checkin' me earlier. Everybody saw you smiling at me."

"You were over there by the couch? Boy, please. You know who I was looking for."

Manny leaned back. "That boy."

"Yeah, Manny. My boyfriend."

You stepped to the right, but he shifted his weight before you could step forward. You turned again and flipped your wrist in his face. He grabbed your arm, twisted it just enough as you pulled away to twist you back in. You wondered, for just a moment, when Manny had gotten so strong. But you came strong, too, got all in his face, even got up on your toes to try to look him in the eye. "Boy you better get offa me."

He hulked over you. Flexed. Flexed like he was dealing with a dude. "What, girl? What? Don't act like that."

You stood your ground, looked out the corner of your eye for him, for your girls, but you stood your ground. "Leave me alone, Manny." You saw the people around you had stopped dancing. Then you thought you saw that other girl smirk, shake her head, then disappear.

Your girls came all at once, like one had gotten the other, and the two had gotten the third. Like they had been dancing right by each other. They all lined up beside you, hands on hips, heads cocked to the side. Ready. You raised your eyebrows at Manny. "Now what?"

But he wasn't paying attention to you anymore. The DJ turned the music off, and he heard the boys from the couch, "yo yo yo yo!" Then Manny sensed the scuffle behind him, felt it aimed at him. Knew he was some other boy's target. He turned, reflexively, turned fast with one arm to block, the other to throw, and, as he turned, knocked you down. His arm cocked as he twisted and hit you so you fell against the credenza, almost to the ground. Your girls reached to catch you,

4

and you felt Shelley pulling you up. "You ok, girl?" and "Dag, Manny" from your girls and "oooooo" from the crowd.

Manny turned back, looked surprised to see you down, reached his hand out to touch you, opened his mouth to speak. Just then his body buckled forward and back at the same time. Someone had jumped on Manny from behind, knocking his body forward, and yoked his neck, driving him back. The yoke pulled strongest, and Manny arched, arms flailing, grabbing up and over for the head of the person behind him. The force behind pulled him into the crowd. Folk parted, girls screamed, "fight! fight!" someone yelled, and boys circled close so you couldn't see what was going on. But you knew. You knew who it was pulling Manny. Who else would it be?

Girls were dashing up the stairs, trying to get out. Someone hit the basement light. You blinked in the sudden brightness. "Yo yo—yo yo!" The DJ yelled into the microphone, "Yo, increase the peace, ya'll. Chiiiiillllll!" Now you could see it was Big Head Hector at the turntables. "Yo, watch my crates, man!"

You heard the pounding above your head. One father and two uncles pounded down the steps. "Ya'll take this mess outta my house!" Manny yoked again, this time by a man twice his size. Dragged up and thrown out.

Everyone pounded up behind them. You knew he'd be in that crowd. You knew it wasn't over.

Your head would have hurt if you stopped long enough to feel it. You saw that other girl, hair wild, sitting on the couch. Her friends were all around her, but you could see her there. She was crying a little and shaking her head. Your eyes locked for a moment, just a moment. No smirk. The room fell silent in that moment. Your crew watching hers and her crew watching yours. But there was no smirk, and you turned around and bolted up the stairs, felt Shelley, Tara, and Michelle behind you.

A few people stood around upstairs, mostly grown-ups now, the father, the two uncles, and the mother. Some cousins. All the family of the girl throwing the party that night. People who were there to make sure nothing like this happened. She looked at you. "But it was my graduation party," she was saying.

You ran through the kitchen.

You could hear the chatter outside before you even made it to the back doorway. Noise that quieted down when you appeared. The quiet was a way for people to take notes, to take in everything so they could talk about it later, so they could say, "I saw . . . I was there."

It was too calm outside. The back alley was too quiet. You knew right away he wasn't out there. No one would have been paying that much attention to you if he were. You felt your body tense, felt yourself stop breathing. You knew it was more than a fight. Just then, you knew.

You twisted back inside, speed walked to the front door. "What she lookin' at you like that for?" Tara whispered loud enough for everybody to hear. The mother stepped forward, hands on hips. "Uh uh," she said. "Ya'll got to go out the back."

"But—"

"But nothin'." She twisted her wrist as she stretched her arm out and pointed. "That way." She put her hand on your back. "Ya'll go on home, now. Just go on home."

"Dag." Tara and Michelle stomped their feet as they turned. Shelley just grabbed you by the arm and pulled you back toward the kitchen.

"I don't want to call the police on these kids, but I ain't havin' all that nonsense out in front of my house," you heard as you let yourself be pulled.

But you were running now. You broke away from Shelley and you were running through the alley. Feet pounded behind you. "Come on, ya'll!" You heard someone call. Shelley, Tara, and Michelle got lost in the crowd. You were running ahead of them all. A mass of flesh and flying sweat followed you now. Individuals bonded in their pursuit. You would have started to feel their pursuit, feel like prey, if you had been thinking, had stopped to think. But for you, the pounding bodies could have been a trail of dust, fumes, fog.

As you turned the corner you could see the rest of the people from the party—another crowd was way ahead of you. You called his name into the night air, into the warm air that was still burning your lungs, making you choke as you ran so hard. Some people turned as you called, but most were focused forward. You could hear yelling, some folk were instigating, some trying to break it all up. You called his name again as you kept running and more people turned, moved out of your way, jumped up and down to try to see. You were at the edge of the crowd now, and people were moving out of your way. You were almost there, could almost see him, called his name again, ran still, ran right into the middle of it, ran right into it as you heard that sound, that sound you had heard before and would hear again.

pop pop pop
Such a simple sound.
pop pop pop
You heard as you ran into the light.
pop pop pop

You heard as you ran into the light, reaching to stars so far, yearning for him so strong, you were reaching to stars that night, and you fell, headlong into a white light blinking bright, then dull, then bright again, above.

"Crystelle Clear?"

Remember.

Chapter One

Darkness resonated in an upward spiral, pushing away the past. She could hear the silence. Then she heard the school-yard across the street, the traffic, her alarm. She reached out to press down, to quiet the nearest noise, and turned over in her bed, slept soundly for a few moments. And then sudden blare reverberated, reached a certain consciousness, hovering like a bone chilling fog where spirals stemmed. Crystelle opened her eyes, saw nothing, then closed her eyes again. Mist clearing. She threw her hands over her face, listened to the music, and the laughter, and the time.

Timelessness shifted places with now as soon as Crystelle opened her eyes. So when her lids drifted down, all she could see was the office where she sat and tried to sell hot chemicals for Black women to pour over their hair. Relaxers. She needed to get ready to go to work. She pulled the covers over her head. She had to go to work. Now she could see the pile of old ad copy on her drafting table. That campaign was over, but a new one would be starting soon. She would have to meet with clients early next week. She would have to do some research, come up with new ideas. What should the model say while she rolls her neck to sell the stuff that straightened hair like hers?

'Post that question in your mind,' she whispered into the crushed fold of white sheets. Shadows against light rose walls flickered to the rhythm of wind. Lace lifted and hard wood floors creaked and Crystelle's sigh echoed.

She rose and dressed and left her building, but she had gathered only enough strength to get to the roar of trains charging toward her underground. With the rush of old air, Crystelle raised her head and looked down into the dark subway tunnel. As a train approached, she backed up, feeling the grime she couldn't see as it landed on her face, stuck to her lipstick. She wanted to lick. She wanted to use her tongue to get the dirt off her lips but she reached for a tissue instead. Against the dash of bodies moving off and on, the dirt and rogue-stained tissue in her hand, Crystelle stood still. Grime against waxy red against white, and the crush of flesh annoyed her. Too much. Too much like what had been. She backed away from the closing doors and turned. Turned away from the pile of ads and the check each pile brought. Away from the stacks of Black women in two-dimensional gloss selling products, away from the money she earned so she could buy them. Turned toward home. As the train lurched forward, Crystelle was already heading toward the stairwell. She could see herself: 'Climb back to the street. Call in sick. Lie in bed, and be sick.' She knew she could get past the noisy schoolyard, through the late-rushing traffic, and climb the brownstone steps. She could climb the carpeted stairs, too, unlock her own door, walk the hard wood, maybe even sleep.

So Crystelle walked across the street with her head held high but her spirit low. So low it gathered bits and flecks of earth as she walked. Against the weaving traffic she saw patterns of steel and exhaust shift. Clouds of smoke and shifting hulks of metal whirred. A man was selling incense on a folding table. Past that, another man was selling videotapes and winter hats. Beyond them all, a man was selling God through a portable microphone. She walked across the street and back into her apartment and there she could lock the door. Her spirit sat down beside her and her head hung low now. It hung so low she could see the flecks and bits caught in the hems of her spirit's skirt. She picked them out. Scooping with her nails like a rake, she gathered the dirt her spirit gathered and she tasted it. So much soil clinging to her disconnected self. Now on her own fingers. Now in her own self. She pressed the gathered earth against her tongue and swallowed the metallic smack of no longer living, of so much decomposed flesh and leaf fertilizing soil. Even in New York City, she could taste death feeding land everywhere. Suddenly she knew the very reason why people pray before putting food into their mouths, the primal instinct to somehow bless this plate of everyday sacrifice.

'Remember this,' her disconnected self said out loud in her head. 'Life feasts on death.'

It would stay inside her forever that taste—of so many slaughtered for sustenance—and she flicked the earth out of her nails and into the Ziploc bag. It held so much. Flowers that were really weeds that were no longer dried but really curled and withered. Stiff and hard, too. She spied the wallet-size photo, yellowed and torn on the edges, that she had stashed so many years ago. Dirt fell out of her own nails and along the treated paper. His image peered out at her, smiling wide, mouth open like the smiler was singing a promise song she couldn't hear because his sounds were muted by the clear plastic.

Crystelle's life began when she was born. But it began again when he died. He was Jimmie, and for all the love she had inside herself to give, much of it poured in from him. She had carried around the weight of his life, the heavy weight of his death.

Everything that had ever been on Frazier Street was a

dream. The place where he grew to die. Home. The memories fell like rainwater—sometimes just a drop, clear, but small. Sometimes, the dream fell so hard, so fast, the wind so strong, it hurt. Crystelle was dreaming whenever she closed her eyes. She shifted from the now to the then. There was no bridge from where she had loved to where she lived. Nothing existed between the two.

She closed the drawer holding the Ziploc bag. Everything her life had been in the beginning and everything it would be in the end was right there.

With him gone, she'd surrounded herself with someone else. It was time to think about what had been and what would be. The truth was sometimes hard to believe: that after everything that had happened in her life, there was still more to be. When Hamp came into her life, she thought nothing much. But that he was still around, poking and probing her spirit, was something to consider. It worked in his favor even if nothing else did—but much more did, even though it still felt like too little. And that meant she would have to consider. What would be enough?

She stood and stripped and collapsed on her bed, and her spirit fell down inside her. In and out of sleep, back and forth in time, she lay still and hot. In the place between wake and sleep she tried to move, tried to simply open her eyes, but her spirit was too low now, and she was, of course, alone.

Hamp would be at work, thinking of her (he said he did), but probably not calling (too busy, too busy till afternoon—sometimes evening, sometimes night). Everyone except her colleagues at the agency would think she was working, too.

She whispered, "I want to wake up now," so out of sleep cycled ahead of her slumber. She lifted both eyelids. Lashes parted and, for a moment, Crystelle started counting the tiny hairs. Then she remembered that was impossible. "I can't do

that," she whispered, and she couldn't. Her brown knuckl[es] turned almost white in the next space of time—almost sev[en] minutes. She knew because she counted each tick against h[er] wall as she gripped air in her hands. "That's six minutes an[d] thirty-two seconds," and she turned her neck, blinked focused, and eyed the rhythmic hand, the one counting eac[h] second against the face of the deep-wood clock. "Brown, whooshed out of her cracked lips, and the second-hand bureau, the smoky glass mirror, the four posts in each corner of the white bed, all the possessions that she'd gathered in Brooklyn loomed into view. She blinked at the nightstand she found on the sidewalk right outside her home one morning. She had been gazing out her six-foot living room window, sipping tea. 'Why would anyone throw it away?' she thought again, reaching out to follow rough patterns, the grain in the wood, with her fingers. She held her hand against a circle, a knot someone had smoothed into a ring. She traced the edges with her thumb. "I can't count anymore," going around.

Clear beads formed everywhere, her skin spit bubbles. The "City of Brotherly Love" shirt, damp, exposed her left breast, where she was burning. She remembered paying a South Street vendor for the T-shirt. He was the guy, he'd said, who crossed out "Love," silk-screened "Shove." It really read "The City of Brotherly Shove." Crystelle had laughed at that. She remembered laughing and the man's eyes slanting into hers, crinkled and blue.

A cloud of mist rose out of the wet ring near her heart Breezes blew, pushing the mist back. Crystelle closed her eye because she was so tired, but she opened them again when sh[e] heard a little boy laughing. Then she fell asleep, and in the slee[p] she saw more, heard herself wheeze. Jimmie danced from fa[r] away, danced up to her and stood, laughing, so close she coul[d] touch him. But she couldn't touch him. They never touched.

"Hey, now."

Talk to me.

"What you want me to say?" She smelled cocoa butter and sweat, and his skin glowed through the dim haze and she knew she was asleep again. It was a dream she knew was a dream just as it was happening. But Crystelle had never smelled Jimmie before—after. Ever since the terrible night and his passing, ever since the dreams began, she could hear him, see him, but never touch. And never smell—until now. Crystelle breathed in deep, even in her dream, and inhaled the cloud of Old Spice poised above her own quiet face. She opened her mouth to ask him about the new sense he was sending her, but Jimmie's words rushed in first.

Talk about you. I wanna hear all about you.

"What about me?"

He grinned.

Silly, start from the beginning. You gotta start from before.

"I gotta start from when?"

Start with Aunt Opal.

"Ma—?"

Yeah.

Crystelle thought about her family while the curtains lifted and fell, lifted and fell, lifted and fell nine times. She could smile, thinking about home, and she licked her lips. A water glass rattled against the hard wood under her bed. For a moment that was all she could see. The water glass and a slip of white paper loomed into view, and then, Jimmie's brown face flashed red.

Now.

"My mamma met my daddy, fell in love, and sneaked him in the house whenever my Granddaddy would leave for more than a minute. As a consequence, I was born, and Mom was forced to marry what Granddaddy would call a three-legged

monster. Of course the marriage didn't last, and although my parents never did get a formal divorce, Daddy moved out before I was old enough to make a memory of him living there. He kind of tripped into my life whenever Mamma needed money for me, and then he would stumble out again, waving as he turned the corner on Frazier and Twenty-sixth Streets. All this sneakin' and leavin' and lovin' went on right there on the same West Philly street I grew up on and moved out of, and—"

—You moved out of—

"Yes."

And it's all going on down there right now.

"As a child I was a part of what made Frazier Street alive."

We.

"We. We made it alive."

You. You made it out alive. We were part of making Frazier Street alive. You made it out alive.

"Yes."

Go on.

"The long, narrow houses were lined up along the kind of pavements only conscious neglect could produce. Both sidewalk and street carried the cracked scars of ice and sun."

I remember.

"Yes."

Go on.

"Nappy-headed boys shot pebbles and chunks of broken asphalt at the feet of us girls as we played our game: double dutch. The few that could aim and hit our dancing feet with more than a lucky shot should have become major league pitchers."

Yes!

"Yes."

Go on.

"We were good and fast. If someone had tied fans to our

feet while we jumped, the wind we would have stirred would have been enough to blow all the autumn leaves off of Frazier Street."

That is, if Frazier Street ever had trees.

"Yes."

Go on.

"Stop interrupting."

You're not remembering right. You're forgetting.

"Stop interrupting."

Go on.

"The hawk came early in West Philly back in the day anyway, so double dutch was mostly a summer sport. The sidewalks couldn't hold a crew of wild sisters like us. So we took over the street itself, moving only for the occasional car. I'd bend forward, ready to slip beneath the moving ropes, and I'd grab hold of the key tied around my neck by one of Granddaddy's old shoestrings. It was especially important to hold tight to that clanky thing once puberty hit and what Granddaddy called my raisin brans started to get in the way. Blurred arms swish-swished the rope, and we'd dive in singin' and doin' our thing:

> Mamma in the kitchen,
> cookin' rice.
> Daddy in the alley,
> Shootin' dice.
> Baby in the cradle,
> Fast asleep.
> Now here comes sister with the
> H-O-T!

And I was hot. I mean, I could work it like no other. When I jumped, people stopped what they were doing and watched.

Neighborhood grandmothers stepped out on their porch now and then, when they got tired of cookin' and cleanin' for three floors worth of family. The sages called out to me like they were in church: 'Go on, girl! Do it!' Instead of Sunday hats, their heads were covered with scarves and head rags. And instead of shaking hymnals and Bibles, they moved brooms, mops, and cooking spoons through the air to the rhythm of my feet on the steaming sidewalk. Flab hung down and also wobbled to the beat from arms fattened by the same tradition of genius that turned the feet of a pig into a culinary classic.

Your granddaddy always said that.

"Mmm."

He always said we could take pig guts and turn it into a culinary classic. Turn around a few generations later and charge folk to eat 'em. Always said that was genius.

"Yes. I got that from him."

Humph. Go on.

The smell of pork filtered out of most of the screen doors on Frazier Street. It wrapped itself around the fried chicken and greens that the summertime air carried each evening, calling us off the street and home for dinner faster than any mamma with promises of a good whipping.

I'd make plans for tomorrow with my friends, throw a pebble or two back at one of the nappy-heads, and jump the stairs by twos up to the front door, cracking paint chips snapping under my sandals.

You hit me once.

"Huh?"

With a rock—you hit me on the side of my head.

"Good for you, then." Crystelle tried to laugh.

Ain't funny.

She licked her lips.

Go on.

"The front porch was screened in. Grandpop usually sat there smokin' and talkin' a lot of stuff to no one in particular.

How's he doing?

"Fine. Better. Stronger."

I should visit him too.

"Mmm."

Go on.

"If he felt the notion, he could lay out full length on the faded green sofa Mamma had set for him each summer. His skinny body would leave enough room for three nice-sized people to sit comfortably, if they sat on the edge down by his legs, and he could still enjoy full view of the little black-and-white TV Mamma had also set up for him."

" 'Come here, girl.' I'd go reach down to give my grand-daddy a hug. He'd prop himself up a bit on his pillow, maybe cough a little from the cigarettes."

" 'Crystelle, was that you? Come on now to dinner.' Mamma'd come walking from the back of the house, wiping her hands on her apron."

" 'Can't a man talk to his granddaughter before he sits down to eat his meal? Don't you start no stuff with me now, girl. Go on back in that ol' kitchen of yours and I'll call you when I'm ready.' "

" 'Daddy, you couldn't call me from the next room much as you been smokin' all your life. Now how you gonna call me from the kitchen?' "

" 'You just go on back in there. And don't worry, you'll hear me when I want you to.' "

"Mamma'd turn to go but would give me a look that said: 'Get up and wash that filth off your face and arms before you dirty up my clean house, young lady. We're about to eat.' "

" 'Well, Granddaddy, I'll be right back. Lemme go pee.' "

" 'Yeah, you go on and pee and then get back down here and

talk before a man eats his meal.' I'd be running upstairs by now to wash for supper."

"Music and laughter from the older kids—"

Manny and them.

"Yes."

Go on.

"Mmm."

You still vexed by him, girl?

"Mmm."

It's okay. I got somethin' for him still. Go on.

"I—"

I said go on.

"Music and laughter from the older kids who could still stay on the street drifted through the bathroom window, as I watched the yellowed sink slowly slurp up the dirty water. I was obsessed with myself and the bathroom mirror, with how I looked."

You were beautiful. Bright, round eyes. Full lips. Full nose. Full—phat.

"Huh."

Go on, baby.

"A thick plait stuck out of an oversized barrette behind the puffy hair on my head. My lips still stung from the salt of sunflower seeds I ate earlier that day. My skin glowed from the heat that kept Granddaddy on the front porch and the fans turned on all day. The bathroom and my bedroom had windows, which should have meant we had a sunnier house than most of our neighbors. We had to keep the shades down most of the time, though. They worked with the fans to keep us cooler in the summer heat, but more importantly, they shielded us from any roaming eyes in the alley outside. So the shades flapped against the windowsills, as the fans turned from side to side, moving the thick air and the dust. We left the curtains in the front room open, though. Granddaddy was from down south, and he said he would never live like a man with a past and hide in his own home. In his special room, the sun always streamed in, the neighbors checked in and out as they pleased, helping Mamma take care of him with their company."

"Once I'd finished looking at myself and eavesdropping on the high school kids, I'd walk across the hardwood floors and down the stairs. Mamma and Granddaddy usually would have started grubbing by then. I'd have to say my own grace and try to catch up. We'd lean on the rusty colored tin and chrome TV trays, the glow from the black-and-white set slowly becoming the only light in the room. It blinked and waved at Granddaddy and me babble on, me talking about all the exciting things I did that day, and Granddaddy about all the exciting things he saw me do. Night crept onto the end tables, and the keen features of a few generations of Southerners and Southerners-moved-North by the boll weevil and a lynch mob or two melted into the growing dark. 'Bless this House' and 'The Lord's Prayer' offered their last chance for a quick reading before also going to sleep on the wood-paneled walls. Mamma would lean back on the pine-green armchair that everyone who walked to the second door of the house had to maneuver around.

Granddaddy wanted his visitors right where he could see them when he was lying down enjoying their company and where they wouldn't have to go too far when he was ready for them to leave. Mamma'd prop her feet up on the heavy wood table, tuck her cotton skirt between her legs, and sip her beer. Granddaddy would lay back to burp, and I'd put my head down at the other end of the couch, closer to Mom, sometimes hoisting my feet up on top of the back of the couch against the wall. We'd watch a few sitcoms whose jokes weren't that funny about people whose lives weren't anything like ours. After the news, Mamma would take Granddaddy upstairs to bed, and I'd go to the kitchen with a handful of plates to wrap leftovers and wash dishes."

"By the time I'd finish and Mamma would have put Granddaddy and herself to bed, even the older kids had gone in for the night. The dark, brick homes, all tight and cozy along Frazier Street, would close their eyes. Street lamps glowed brighter than the moon. I'd fall asleep under the artificial haze that managed to mesh through my window shade, the whir of the fans and Granddaddy's snoring lulling me away. My room was my place in the world, which was movin' right out there on Frazier Street the next morning with the cockle-doodle-doo of a garbage truck. 'Till then, Frazier Street was still sleeping, snoring even— after all, it was alive."

Back in the day.

Crystelle looked up at Jimmie smiling down at her.

Baby, that was so nice.

Her eyes gleamed, and she was silent for a while.

You changin' your voice and telling a real story like that. Using real story words. That was so nice.

Crystelle thought she saw his teeth. "Oh, Jimmie," she heard, long and high and fading now, as mist rolled, blowing him away.

* * * *

Frustrating herself, she tried to move, to sit up, but the sleep became too deep, too consistently deep, and her spirit was too low. She gave up and just lay. The silence settled down on top of her, on top of the dispirited image that followed her everywhere. For the first time in a long time she slept hard and long. The sleep lasted until a moon started rising just outside her window, the sun still streaking last light through sky.

Crystelle rose in the near dark of a side street in Brooklyn, to a car alarm on the street. She splashed her face, looked in her refrigerator, and lay herself down again. She thought about reading, and then she thought about watching TV. She sighed and turned over and sighed and turned over again. She thought about Hamp thinking about her, and slowly she started to touch herself. She could see him rocking to the lurch and throw of the express to Brooklyn. The feeling of him rocking could enter her, if she touched and thought hard enough. But only the stillness of rose-colored quiet settled and shifted and settled again as she stroked herself slightly. She sighed and turned over and sighed and turned over again, thinking about not seeing him that night. The telephone was so close she could reach with her hand and touch it, make her way through the wires twisted into tangles. The cordless Hamp bought her once a long time ago was still wrapped and packed in the original box somewhere in her hall closet. She'd never activated voice mail, even though he gave her cash to pay for one full year. In the near dark of the empty night she reached and clicked the jack with her finger and thumb. But that didn't work.

Time gathered onto itself, but Crystelle heard Hamp turn his key in her door before time could shift. She heard it as she moved from the lightest sleep to awake, before she journeyed anywhere in time. She shook away the haze, and the thinnest beginnings of white fog and mist disappeared. So she sat up and then lay back not thinking. Then she turned on the light next to her bed.

Hamp walked in without speaking and smiled. He just stood and smiled and looked at her lying in the bed, nearly naked, not thinking. He smiled and showed his teeth, and Crystelle remembered how much she loved his teeth. They were strong and even and white against his brown face. She wondered if his mother had breast-fed him. She was about to ask when he lay down on the sheet on top of her, so she closed her mouth and decided to wait and ask him later. Maybe she wouldn't ask him at all. She would ask the dentist if breast milk gave a baby healthier teeth later on. Or she could ask her doctor once she became pregnant some day. Right now he was moving on top of her and rubbing his face against the sheet on top of her in the bed. That was something. She would have to do something.

She pulled off his jacket and then his shirt and tie, and she wondered if he had thought to take his shoes off before he came in. He got up on his knees, and as she reached for his pants, she peeked to see. He had. That was something. He liked it when she bent down to take off his shoes for him, but she didn't feel like it. Not tonight. Tonight she just wanted to lie back and feel him on top of her and not really have to do too much. She would make it up to him later. He knew to take off his shoes, and that night he moved like he knew she just wanted to kind of lie still and feel him on top of her and inside her, and for her, that was something, too.

She reached up for his hair, remembering how much she had once loved his hair, but all she felt was the close cut of his corporate look. She missed the soft feel of his almost locks when they first met in college. His high top fade grew out into something substantive by the time they were graduating, something she could reach out and hold onto. She would lay back with his head in her lap, pulling each lock, counting his locks, losing herself in the pulling and counting, never quite counting them all. But now his hair, close-cut corporate, almost cut her if she rubbed her face against his head. She missed his round eyes following her from underneath high-top locks. She missed having something to hold onto, when she slid her hands from his face to his ears and along the back of his neck to his hair.

She could lie there and close her eyes and not think now

that he was in and on top of her. She could be there feeling him but not really be there too, and that felt good enough that night. She didn't have to make much noise; she could just enjoy the still quiet and his slow rhythm. She didn't know why this was what she wanted, why this was all she wanted that night. Maybe the moon was almost full. She opened her eyes to look through the lace blowing against her window. She looked past his suit, stripped and formless now against her red, velvet chair, past his keys tossed on her nightstand.

She looked out for the moon, not thinking about anything but the moon and if it was full that night. Light cast down and up through the shade on her lamp. The trick of light made her blink. A crackle and pop glittered just above a whisper in the corner of her room, and she blinked again. The sound of wind streaming through still air tickled her eyelashes, raised the hair in the nape of her neck. Unseen movement circled under her chin, snaked her whole head. Crystelle wrapped her arms around Hamp, stretched one arm down the rise and fall of his back to pull him close. He groaned and pulled and pushed against the air above them both, so Crystelle knew he didn't hear the whispering light. She closed her eyes and heard a snap that nearly blinded her—even in the darkness of her own shut face—and a sound with no shape came out of her own body. Her sound with no meaning echoed for three beats against the walls of her bedroom. For three beats of sound, her furniture, his keys, everything disappeared but Hamp, the echo, and her own flailing arms. She tried to look up again but beads of heat bubbled and rolled down the great width of Hamp's shoulder, along the deep cut of muscle, and splashed into her right eye. First one, then another, then again. She blinked and squinted and slowly felt herself focus past her lover. In the angle of light and dark against the ceiling she saw shade. Another groan came out of her own body, another sound with no form that didn't mean anything. The shade reverberated to the rhythm of her meaningless cry. That made her neck roll, and she looked to the right on her bed because she wanted to make sure no one was sitting cross-legged beside her and Hamp. Light fell in against almost darkness, and she looked up again to see what shadows stood. When Crystelle lay with her lover that night, she looked up and counted three outlines against the plaster, hovering above her bed.

"But he only comes when I fall asleep," she tried to say as Hamp thrust deeper, and all she could do was groan. Crystelle's sobs and shakes were for both of them that night, the one who was alive, and the other, the one who had left and then had somehow come back to her.

When she shivered, Hamp thought it was because of him, so he made himself finish, lay against her for a minute, kissed her face, said love you in her ear, then rolled over to sleep. He never felt her quiet scream against his own. He felt so tired. He never noticed Crystelle lay awake most of the night, staring without thinking above her bed. He was so tired.

Chapter Two

Day rose up and out through the sky. Crystelle's eyes opened before Hamp's and she closed hers again. She was happy to sleep longer, to rest with his body next to hers. Sometimes at night she could open her eyes and look into his eyes looking at her. She could look into his because he lay so close looking at her into the night. This morning, she could breathe and feel his breathing and match his breathing, his breath. She could stretch on her side of the bed and he could stay on his and they could still be close. It was nice. It helped the night before drift. It almost helped her forget.

Crystelle must have dozed off because she woke with Hamp on top of her again. With his lips on her face and his love in her ear, she moved her body with his.

"My woman," he said.

"Put a condom on," she whispered back. He moved some more and she lay still and then he did. And then she moved again and slowly, slowly she let her body reach his, and it was like breathing in the earliest morning. She figured it was nice, but she really had little else to compare it to, so it being nice was kind of a guess.

That morning as Crystelle lay still in the quiet and Hamp lay breathing to his own rhythm now, she heard the kitchen phone ring. She reached up and out so fast—glad for a reason to turn from the space above her bed——that she plugged in the phone before the machine clicked on.

Crystelle tugged the phone jack, felt the tangle pull into an almost ball, and picked up her phone. Her mother spoke a sentence or two before Crystelle could mumble "I'll call you later." It was too soon for the sound of her mother's voice.

"Baby, that was so nice," Hamp whispered. "You got me so open," he laughed, before he rolled over her, off of her, and into the bathroom to pee. Crystelle peeked up at the ceiling one last time, but it was bright morning, and she couldn't even see her own shadow. She closed her eyes until he crawled back into her bed and put his arm over her body, his hand on her stomach. He reached over to turn off the light. Then he put his arm on her stomach again.

"Marry me," he whispered.

"Boy, please."

"Sure, we might have a boy first."

"Come on, Hamp."

"I did already."

"Hamp, don't talk like that."

"Like what? You can do it but you can't talk about it after?" He slapped her hip and pulled her body full length and facing him. He traced her face, kissed her nose, looked a *you mine, girl* deep into her soul. She felt the lovelove pour from his eyes. Her spirit sat up inside her, palms open, cupped, spread to catch his feeling in her.

"Hamp, you believe in ghosts?"

"What?"

"You believe in spirits?"

"You mean haints, charms, spells, and the ancestors knocking on your door late past midnight?" Hamp laughed and stretched out before looking back at Crystelle. "What's that question all about?"

"Just wanna know—do you believe?"

A light breeze skipped through the just cracked bedroom window. The lace curtains Hamp loved—the ones that made Crystelle's room look girlie, like a woman's, his country gal—rose and fell and rose. The lace pattern danced across her deep-brown face as midmorning sun sent light, warming her room. He traced the dancing lace pattern against her cheek with his eyes. Hamp felt his half groan bounce in the silence of his look-ing, as he pulled Crystelle even closer and closed his eyes.

Crystelle felt his strength in the morning—the power of his pulling and looking and groaning and not answering. She felt it comfortable but she also felt it unanswered. He felt big and protective and just big at the same time. She lay there without moving until he started breathing deeper. Then she eased out from under his arm and thought about her own shadows and her own dreams. 'What if those were Jimmie's eyes all along?' She was thinking about middle of the night eyes and had an almost answer when she felt Hamp toss and reach out and pull her close again. She squirmed and Hamp opened one eye side-ways at her.

"What's up?"

"Ummm, hungry?"

He turned over on his stomach and yawned. Crystelle reached out and rubbed his back.

"Hungry?"

A big noise that sort of said yeah fell out with his next yawn.

Crystelle rose to slip on her bathrobe and walked into the kitchen. She looked back one time, as she walked through her living room, just glancing once at the doorway to her bed-room before she turned and entered her kitchen. There space squeezed in on her, as she twisted and turned from the brown Frigidaire to the deep sink. In the tiny countertop space, she chopped onions, grated cheese, and cracked eggs while turkey bacon popped above the only flame that would light on her gas stove. She made enough for three, and, as she pulled two plates from the cabinet, realized she still didn't want to eat.

Hamp walked in just as she was putting her plate back into the wall. He pulled her the two inches it took to get her hips right where he wanted them—between him and the tiny counter. As he kissed her neck, she let her hand drop, and he ran his fingers along the length of her arm to grab the plate from her.

"Whatchu puttin' this back for?" he breathed down the silk against her skin.

"I'm not hungry," she whispered back. Her hair fell forward along her face, and suddenly Crystelle could feel it all—the silk in her bathrobe, his palms, the edge of the tiny counter, his rise against her lower back, space within her opening up on itself, adjusting her legs against him. He turned her around and made her look up and into his face. He smiled, and she could feel her legs realign along the new rhythms pouring out from her and into his hand. He kissed her eyes, and as she looked down again, he grabbed her earlobe with his teeth.

"You gotta eat, baby."

Crystelle tried to slip to the side, but the kitchen was too small for her to get far.

He wrapped one free arm around her waist and used his other hand to guide her back against him. "Look up here." She felt his hand below her belly so strong it lifted her chin.

"Like that?" he teased. "I got you like that?"

Crystelle didn't answer so he dug a little deeper and her whole head fell forward. She rubbed her cheek against his arm.

"I got you like what?"

"Like that." She could barely hear her own voice. He sent it so high, it almost disappeared.

He could readjust his hand even more; she pulled back and then fell forward. "How I got you, girl?"

"Like that. Just like that, Hamp."

"You gotta eat, baby."

Crystelle just fell against his whole body now. Her whole body against his. He pulled himself out of her, pulled her hair to bring her face up to his, kissed her eyelashes.

"You gonna eat something this morning."

"MmHm."

"Fill these plates, Crys. Don't lose what you got."

"MmHm."

He pulled back and stepped to the side as Crystelle leaned over and filled one plate, then another.

"You trying to say I'm losing too much weight?"

"MmMm. Here." Hamp spooned the rest of the omelet onto her plate, picked up both, and walked over to the wood table. "Sit down."

Crystelle walked over and sat.

"You want orange or cranberry?" he called from inside the ice box as he pushed aside the humus, salsa, pita, and grapes.

"Both. Mixed. Most men would be glad to have their significant other keeping it trim."

"I don't know the brother that doesn't want the booty big." Hamp kissed the back of her neck again as he put her juice in front of her. "Here you go."

He looked at his food and mouthed a silent prayer for himself, then he ate and ate. He didn't notice Crystelle mostly pushed and pulled the food against her plate. He didn't notice that she threw most of her food away. He was so hungry.

She was stacking the dishes in the sink when he walked in tying his tie.

"Where're you going, Hamp?"

"Gotta go in for a while this morning."

"I thought we would be together all day."

"Gotta make the money, honey. Gotta get this deal done."
He kissed her on the cheek as he adjusted the knot against his
throat.

"It's Saturday." She watched him pick up his cell phone. "I
thought we could have time to talk." She watched him point
one finger in the air and then use it to press the numbers on his
keypad.

"Gotta check my messages, baby."

Crystelle turned to wash the dishes. The sink filled with
white bubbles, and she felt the steam curl the broken ends of
hair framing her face.

"What did you say, sweetie?" Hamp flipped his phone into
the briefcase and snapped the locks.

"Nothing." She fixed her face and looked up into his.

"It's not like I want to go in."

"I know."

He kissed her other cheek and left, and even though Crystelle had enough to do, she went back to sleep. The hot dish-
water turned cold. It would take late morning and early
afternoon for Crystelle to rise again. She opened her window
wide, and the sounds from a playground's worth of children ran
up to her face. The sun fell hard and fast. School had started but
autumn hadn't; it was Indian Summer. Crystelle longed for the
cool of fall. A real fall with crunchy leaves, smooth tea, and big,
warm sweaters. Crystelle wanted a real fall. She longed for the
change. Somehow, from there as a child to here as a woman,
things had stayed the same.

She had been rocking along the Saturday breeze all morning. Now she stood up, really awake. She needed to wash the
sheets on her bed. She needed to dust and she needed to call
her mother. She tied her shoulder length hair up in a tight bun
and rubbed a cloth over the nightstand and dresser she'd found

at the Park Slope flea market her first week in Brooklyn. Then she wiped down the bookshelf, desk, and coffee table she'd U-Hauled from a Philly sale. The light wood in the living room kept her apartment airy. The dark in her bedroom helped her feel cozy. She threw her bathrobe into a pile of whites, slipped into sweats, and ran out of her apartment and downstairs to the basement laundry room. Then she decided to wash down her kitchen and the bathroom too.

Crystelle knew the dusting and cleaning were a preparation. She knew she would be leaving soon. The pull of going was strong now. Labor Day weekend she had lain back on the stony sand at The Inkwell, thinking of stone steps at home. Hamp would reach out and trace lines he made for himself on her bare skin, and Crystelle would let him. She couldn't even be mad at him for not knowing she wasn't feeling his touch, even as she closed her eyes and felt him.

She picked up the phone to call her mother, then she hung up. She picked up her phone to call her office, remembered it was Saturday when her manager's voice mail came on, and hung up. She went to the kitchen, took out cheddar cheese and a box of macaroni, then put it all back. She returned to her bedroom to call Hamp, remembered he was going into his office that morning, and hung up. She lay back on her bed but sat back up again. Crystelle stood up, looked over at her pillows, and walked away from her bed. She picked up the phone on her kitchen wall and called Amtrak. Then she called her manager's voice mail. Then she called home.

"Mamma?"

"Hey, Honey."

"I'm coming home."

"Good."

"I'm coming home tonight."

"You want me to pick you up at the station?"

"I'll catch a cab, cause I get in late."

"How late?"

"10:21."

"I can get you."

"It's okay."

"You off next week?"

"I'm just gonna take off a few."

"You have the days?"

"Yeah. I haven't missed one yet."

"You don't want to use them for some big trip?"

"Nope. I'm coming home."

"You miss your mamma?"

Crystelle laughed with her mother, "Of course."

"I figured you'd be home for this boy's parole hearing. Brenda'll appreciate that, honey. It's Tuesday, right?"

Crystelle had almost forgotten. Manny and them. "Yeah."

"So, I'll see you soon. I looooove you."

"I loooove you, too."

"Okay—Oh, Crystelle!"

"Yeah?" Crystelle brought the phone back to her ear.

"Guess what."

"What?"

"Guess who I had a dream about last night."

"Who?"

"Maybe that's why I had the dream. Couldn't figure it out before, but now, talkin' to you, it makes sense. Must've been thinkin' about the hearing on Tuesday."

"Who, Mamma? Who'd you dream about?"

"Jimmie Johnson."

Crystelle felt the phone slip through her hand. "I've been having dreams, too, Mamma." She didn't even know if the receiver was up by her mouth when she spoke. Then she heard a man's voice, and she gripped it tighter, just before it fell away. "Who's that?"

"I'm coming now. Hello, Crystelle?"

"Hey."

"That was your grandfather."

"Oh."

"I'll see you tonight. You got your key?"

"Yeah."

"All right—"

"Mamma, tell me about the dream."

"Daddy's calling again, Honey."

"Just real quick."

"I don't even think much happened. If it did, I don't remember."

"What do you remember?"

"Him. Just him. I saw him."

"How'd he look?"

"Same. Same as five years ago."

"Oh."

"It was a good face. I mean, nothin' bad wasn't happening."

"Oh."

"It's Crystelle, Daddy!"

"Mamma?"

"She's coming down tonight!"

"Ma."

"Yeah, I'm coming up now!"

"Mommy."

"Girl, let me go get to my father."

"Yeah, I'll see you later."

"Looove you."

"Looove you, too."

Crystelle hung up, sat still for two minutes, felt herself

falling back. Her back arched and her stomach muscles tight-
ened, and just as she felt the soft cotton against her cheek, she
sat up again. She stood. Started moving. By the time she'd put
fresh sheets on her bed, the laundry was done. After a long
shower, she threw a few things in a bag, left a message for
Hamp, and left. As she turned the corner on her block, Crystelle looked up at the row of brownstones behind her. She
moved into Fort Greene because she'd always felt she was
meant to live in a big house like the one she lived in now. When
she signed her lease, she'd promised herself one day she'd be
signing a deed. She didn't know where that feeling came from,
only that she felt she somehow deserved to live like that. She'd
resolved to work and save and make her money, make enough
money for a down payment on one of these big brown buildings. Crystelle almost turned around and walked back to her
one bedroom apartment. She needed to work. She'd missed so
much work, and she needed to work on the ad campaign from
her desk at home. She needed to walk into work on Monday
with a few good ideas and at least one great one. She needed to
make money.

A cool breeze tickled the nape of Crystelle's neck as she
stood there. A few wisps of hair had slipped out of the tight
bun. A child laughed, running through the schoolyard. "You
can't catch me!" she yelled at a boy her age running behind her.
Crystelle pushed her hair up toward the tight knot, turned her
back on the row of historic buildings, and headed toward the C
train.

When she got down into the subway, she felt good. A train
pulled up soon, and Crystelle got a seat. She pulled her bag
onto her lap. Then she looked up and into the face of a stranger
sitting across from her. His face made her think about giggling,
about passing notes in class. He looked like the almost man
Hamp used to be.

Locks fell around his face. His long fingers rested on his thighs, as the train pulled and pushed into the city. His features were long, too. Long but full at the same time. She looked up and across and could see his eyes, closed and still. She could still see into them. His face was just like a mask carved from African wood—she couldn't see the eyes, but the soul was still there. And flesh. Thinking, she thought. He is not thinking, she thought; but, the thoughts flow to him. She knew that look of peace. She had seen it before—that face where thoughts flow in. And rhythm, she thought, the train's rhythm pulls him to and from sleep.

He looked serene to her. She saw him with his thick jeans, thick shirt, thick boots, all flecked with plaster or paint or something white. His face held the secrets of the ancestors, and he did not sway as the train moved. He sat perfectly still. Crystelle realized he didn't look like Hamp did when he was younger. He didn't look like Hamp at all. He looked just like the men she remembered. The men who were young and worked in jeans. So many suits on the trains when she rushed to make nine and five time. . . . Here on a Saturday evening was a man who worked in jeans.

Crystelle thought about being with a man like this one, like the men she had known all along. She knew a man like this would be with a somebody. A woman would be with him. She thought about her. She, too, must be beautiful. Brown, like him. Strong, like him. She works, like him. For the city proba- bly. And in her cubicle, where she sits each day, a snapshot curls against her wall. They knew each other in high school. She goes to college part time. He supports her, thinks of her each day, makes love to her each night. She always has dinner ready. Crystelle could see into his shut face and see it all there. It all existed in the place where she was going now. She had grown up in it. She could see that they would have children soon and things would be different. She had seen that too. Right now he can sit back, stretch, and feel her hips rock him to sleep, even as she clears the kitchen table. She had seen that.

He washes clothes and dishes and cooks. She washes clothes and dishes and cooks. They work. He drinks with his boys and talks about women, thinks about her. She answers the telephone, talks about men, thinks about him. They make love.

He pulls himself out of bed. She pulls herself out of bed. They collapse in the night into arms brown and soft and hard, and working hands touch chipped nails in the dark behind the shades in the night under the blankets they make love. And the pattern is regular, and the pattern is rhythm, and they are not alone when they are together.

Crystelle did not have that, what she could see he had with his woman. It didn't exist in the world she had run into. In the world she occupied now, everyone ran away from that pattern, away from the rhythm of deep love. Where she was, marriage didn't open like a flower in growing light. Where she was, people married just because they had been together for so long. Because they were both making enough money. Because he could afford the right-sized ring in the right color box.

Crystelle looked up when the man across the aisle opened his eyes to rise and walk away from a nearly dilapidated subway tunnel or a nearly finished building, away from a day of double time. She looked up and into his open eyes that barely saw her as she watched him walk out through closing doors. He did not see me, Crystelle thinks, he loves his woman so. He was a promise Jimmie had made to her so long ago. He was a promise for someone like who she had been then. He was a glimpse of what she had thought would be her future. He was what never came to be.

She could look back down and not feel sad. Her man had a love that was strong. She created a face for Hamp—one that reflected contentment. It was hard, and the next stop was hers anyway, so Crystelle rose herself. She stood up like the stranger riding in front of her had. She needed to be alert when she opened her purse to pay for the one way ticket. She had to watch the big board, trying to anticipate which tunnel the train bound for Philadelphia would pull into. Then she had to rush.

She could rush without the thrill of adrenaline—it was just a running for the gate. She found a seat easily, and then she remembered it was Saturday night. Only single travelers and a couple or two rode on Saturday night.

She sat in the seat without feeling connected to it. Without feeling connected to anything, she sat and tried to recreate the face of Hamp. She had never seen him look like the man on the subway. The stranger was tired but full of peace. Hamp was always rushed and tired. He looked sideways too much. She could see his face twitch ever so slightly when he made his plans. His look was never calm and deep and still. Crystelle tried to convince herself that it was because of his work, because the numbers never let go of him. He had to take other people's money and make money off of theirs, as if it was his own. It made him so rushed all day that even when the rest of him slept in her bed, his face kept moving. "The woman sets the tone of the household." An aunt had told her that once. But they didn't have a household yet.

Never calm, never deep, never still, he would look, but then he would look away. Crystelle took her ticket to the café car. She ordered a hot dog, chips, and soda. The conductor punched her ticket as soon as she sat back down. She smiled because she could look at him and see the black and white of an uncle somewhere in her grandfather's old photo album. He smiled back. "Good to see a good-looking woman eating real food," he said.

Crystelle just nodded, chewed, and swallowed. "It will probably make me sick later," she said.

"Naw. Good for you to eat like that once in a while."

"Maybe," she smiled back.

"You getting off in Philly?"

"Thirtieth Street."

"All right," he smiled in her sleepy eyes before he moved down the aisle.

Crystelle sipped her soda and watched New Jersey flash. All the aluminum siding, a few strip malls, some old warehouses, and the playgrounds. She watched them all flash by. Thinking about Hamp, sort of, she started to think about home. She wondered how many of her friends she would see, since Tara and Michelle had moved. And, of course, Jimmie was gone.

She could close her eyes now. She could leave them open and watch the aluminum siding pass her by in the fading light, or she could close her eyes and see the brick that lines the street back home. She could close her eyes and see clearly the brick and the time when everyone could see everyone else easily. She could close her eyes and see a boy that had gazed into her face, calm and still, making plans. That was what she decided to do. The aluminum had become a blur; but, now, the brick and asphalt and the faces were clear. The back from forth was coming. She could see and she shook, and she turned away from the rush of images outside her window. Then she felt time settle her in sleep. She could look past the stranger loving his woman like she had always figured she would be loved when she was back home. She could look past the conductor that would have reminded Granddaddy of his own back home. Even as she moved forward in a train bound for home, she swayed to sleep and shifted backwards in time. The shift was clear. She saw home in the shift. She saw inside. She could see the past clearly, and then, she was there, even as she slept soundly on the train moving forward toward home. She made herself dream of the past.

* * * *

Crystelle's hand shook as she dug through the plastic container on her white lacquer dresser. Red and blue beads danced from fingertip to fingertip, teasing her. In time, she grasped them all. She looked at her closed hand and felt the beads against her palm. They were real. She hurled herself into her younger self and lost herself in home. She was a girl again. It was a dream that she let carry her spirit out of her own body and into her younger self.

"I'm going to Shelley's now, Mamma, see you later!"

"Yeah, by 8:00 and I mean it!" But Crystelle was already halfway down the front stoop, and she could hear the conversation three houses down better than she could hear her own mother, just a few yards away in the kitchen.

A football rolled point over point down the street. Jimmie followed, running with arms outstretched toward the pavement that the ball was leaving behind. Crystelle laughed at Jimmie as he tried to grasp the ball. He finally did, tucked it under his arm, and side-skipped back up to where Crystelle stood— three houses down and right in front of Shelley's house.

Jimmie grinned at Crystelle and said, "Ya'll know those boys can't throw."

"Looks to me like you can't catch," Crystelle's friend Shelley returned.

"Oh yeah, who's winning?" Jimmie asked, still looking at Crystelle.

"Boy, you know I don't know a thing about football," Shelley replied.

Jimmie laughed a bit and turned up to the steps the three older girls occupied.

"Well, who's winning, Jimmie?" Crystelle cut in.

"Aw, Crystelle, you know I'm on the winning team. As long as you're watching, I'm gonna keep on winning." Jimmie leaned forward to steal a kiss on Crystelle's cheek, then jumped off the curb and ran backward a few steps laughing. "Come on, Crystelle, try and catch me!"

Crystelle just cut her eyes, sucked her teeth, and twisted her wrist in Jimmie's direction. Then she turned quick and marched up to Shelley's steps to sit. Jimmie backed up some more, threw the ball up in the air, and whooped and hollered before he caught it. He played catch with himself all the way up the block and high-fived the other boys, who had been watching and waiting and cheering a little for the stolen kiss.

Crystelle sat on the step in front of Shelley and positioned herself between Shelley's knees. She pulled the front hem of her T-shirt forward to form a pouch and watched the red and blue beads fall from her hand into the cotton basin. She reached behind her ear to hand her comb up to Shelley.

"Here, Crystelle, hold these. They'll keep your stuff together while I fix it," Shelley passed a few hairclips back down to Crystelle. She parted and reparted Crystelle's hair until she got it perfect, straight down the middle.

"Girl, when are you and Jimmie gonna get married?" Shelley teased.

"You don't see me studying Jimmie Johnson," Crystelle said a little too loudly.

"Well, Jimmie Johnson sure is studying you," Tara offered. "Check him." Crystelle looked up (she had been looking down because Shelley was scratching the back of her head just then), and she saw Jimmie holding the football up in the air with one hand and pointing at her with the other. His knees were bent and moving fast.

"Touchdown!" Jimmie told the neighborhood. Crystelle looked back down and let Shelley finish working on her hair. The comb felt good against her scalp. Shelley had a way of making each pull of the comb feel like—

"Queen of Sheba or something." Crystelle startled up to see Jimmie leaning on Shelley's rail.

"All right, girl, you're making me mess up."

"Sorry, Shelley. What did you say, Jimmie?"

"I said you're acting like the Queen of Sheba or something."

"What am I supposed to do, Jimmie? You see I'm getting my hair done."

"You used to cheerlead for me. Right here where now you're just sittin'."

"Cheerlead?"

"Football."

"Oh, I used to play, too, but ya'll got too rough."

"No, uh-uh, Crystelle, you got too soft. You used to want to play tackle on this street."

"Well, my tackle days are over."

"Ya used to cheerlead."

"Boy, that wasn't even real cheerleading. Plus, I didn't like to cheerlead. I liked to play."

"Well you don't do anything now."

"I'm doing something now."

"What are you doing now?—except getting your hair done."

"Nothing."

"What?"

"That's all I'm doing right now—getting my hair done."

"So go on now, Jimmie. All you're doing right now is getting in the way," Tara offered. Shelley gently pushed Crystelle's head down while Tara spoke. She continued combing in the nape of Crystelle's neck.

Jimmie twisted his body, put his face under Crystelle's, and smiled. "Am I in your way, Crystelle? You answer."

"Ow!" The comb had worked into a soft spot in Crystelle's kitchen, but Jimmie kept his face where it was—every feature grinning up at Crystelle.

"You've never been tender-headed before—sorry," Shelley ran her fingers along Crystelle's scalp.

"I'll come by once my hair's finished, okay? Let you see my new 'do," Crystelle smiled down.

Jimmie twisted back up, "Check ya later, then. Bye."

"All right now," Shelley sent after him. She moved the comb from Crystelle's kitchen to the spot behind her right ear, scratching lightly and humming. Crystelle closed her eyes as she leaned back on that slab of concrete step. Each elbow rested on one of Shelley's knees, and she moved her head around slowly from side to side. The perfect part was lost in all the scratching.

Tara stood up, brushing the bottom of her cut-off jeans with the palms of her hands. "I'm goin' to the corner to buy sunflower seeds. Do ya'll want anything?"

"Yeah. Bring me back some Now an' Laters," Crystelle kept turning her head as she spoke.

"I'ma just bum off of ya'll," Shelley said.

"Are you coming, Michelle?" Tara asked.

"Sure." The two walked slowly up the sidewalk.

Shelley prepared Crystelle's hair for braiding. "So, what'cha plan on doing with ol' Jimmie when your 'do is done?"

"Huh?"

"You heard me, Crystelle. What are you going over to his house for?"

"Shelley, I go over to Jimmie's all the time."

"Not when his mom is out of town you don't."

Crystelle had forgotten Jimmie's mother was away for the weekend. "His father is there, Shelley."

"His father works nights."

"Oh, come on. I go over there when he's home alone all the time."

"Maybe. But you never know when someone is gonna pop in most of the time. Tonight you know he's home alone."

"Well, I can't stay out too late anyway."

"It doesn't take too long."

"What doesn't?"

"You know."

"No, I don't know. What?"

"Well, if you have to ask, then you don't need to know."

"I hate it when people say that."

"Just don't be going over there all hours of the night."

"I'm not."

"Pass me a clip."

Crystelle dug in her lap for a hairpin and passed it up to Shelley. She was holding a section of her hair back with the other hand. Her head was cocked to the side, and Shelley began to twist strands of Crystelle's hair section by section until her entire head took on new form. She could feel Shelley's short, wide fingers pull and knuckle and pull down her head. Every so often the fabric hanging from the bow on Shelley's blue halter top would catch a breeze. Crystelle could feel the cotton tickle the backs of her arms. She looked down at her own pink, jelly-bean sandals and Shelley's flip-flops whenever her friend would add two beads and finish a braid.

"So what do you and Jimmie be doing together anyway?"

"Dag."

"Well?"

"Dag, Shelley. We just talk, or watch TV, or sit out on the front and don't say nothing at all."

"Does he call you?"

"Yeah."

"Does he hang out with you at lunch and stuff?"

"Sometimes. Sometimes he just gets on my nerves and I don't speak to him in school."

"I heard he got in a fight with Ray Ray last week."

"Dag."

"What you mean dag?"

"We're not gonna be in high school till next year. How does the junior high news make it to the high school?"

"We all live on the same block, Crystelle."

"Yeah, but that fight wasn't on the block. It was at school. A junior high school. Why ya'll studying us?"

"We are not studying ya'll. Jimmie comes on the bus all loud talking about what he did to who after school. Shoot, he wants people to know he's fightin' for you."

"He was not fighting for me."

"That's what he said."

"Ray Ray and him got into it over some other girl."

"I heard they got into it over you."

"Well, I don't know how. I ain't studying Jimmie Johnson and I sure ain't studying no big head Ray Ray."

"His body'll catch up."

"MmHm."

"Well, Jimmie can't be comin' to West Philly High like he's all that. He's got to start over in high school. He'll be the youngest again."

"Whatever."

"All right."

"I ain't studying—"

"All right."

Tara and Michelle appeared from around the corner. Tara laughing and Michelle singing off-key until they plopped back down on Shelley's steps. They passed around the bag of sunflower seeds, and everyone except Shelley popped them in their mouths one by one. They sucked salt with their tongues, cracked seeds between their teeth, spit shells through O-shaped lips.

"Hey, Tara," Shelley threw in, "tell Crystelle what's it."

"What'cha mean 'what's it,' it who?"

"It what," Shelley corrected.

"It whaa—ohhh, it it."

"As in doin' it?" Michelle giggled.

"In this case, wondering what it." Shelley didn't stop moving her fingers through Crystelle's hair as she spoke.

"You mean as in not doin' it, if it's all about wondering what it," Tara said.

"Shoot, if you're asking . . ." Michelle turned to Crystelle.

"I know—then I don't need to know," Crystelle rolled her eyes. Shelley held the comb in the air and silently mouthed the words along with Crystelle.

"You got it."

"Amen."

"There you go, honey bunch."

"What have ya'll been talking about since we've been gone, Shelley?" Michelle asked.

"Just what Tara said—not doin' it."

"Crystelle is worrying about not doin' it? Humph." Michelle swung around and looked past Crystelle at Shelley, "I don't see where she could feel cause for alarm." Michelle smiled at Crystelle. "It'd take a boy all day just to find those two little stubs you've got trying to stick out under your T-shirt."

Everyone laughed and Shelley started retwisting an errant braid in Crystelle's hair. "Don't ya'll worry. Someone out here is gonna want to go with Crystelle soon enough."

"Uh oh, who likes you, Crystelle?" Michelle asked.

"I don't know," Crystelle mumbled.

"Oh yes she does," Shelley encouraged Michelle.

"Oh, I can find out now," Michelle smiled without showing any teeth this time.

"How?" Crystelle demanded. Then she added, "There isn't any boy to find out about any old way."

"Well, we're gonna see for sure right now." Michelle stood up and walked up the steps toward Shelley's front door. She wiped her hands against the bottom of her red shorts as she took each step.

"What'cha gonna get in my house to help you?" Shelley turned around to look up at Michelle as she spoke.

"Honey, all I need is a piece of paper and a pencil, and I can tell you everything you need to know." Michelle stood at the highest step now.

"All right, then. Look in the kitchen drawer where Grandma keeps her cards." Before Michelle reappeared, Shelley finished one braid and began another.

Michelle emerged with a pad of paper and a magic marker. Crystelle sat leaning forward, as Shelley fixed a bead onto the end of a braid. The pad fell on the step in front of Crystelle when Michelle plopped down.

"All right, what's your favorite number?" Michelle looked up at Crystelle.

"Thirteen."

"That's too big a number," Tara cut in.

"How do you know?" Michelle rolled her eyes toward Tara.

"You're not the only one who knows how to do this. Everybody knows how to work this kind of stuff." Tara rolled her eyes right on back.

"Who's doing it now, though?"

Tara just flipped her hand up and turned her head the other way.

"Crystelle," Michelle continued, "who's doing it now?" Before Crystelle could reply Michelle closed her eyes, gave her head a quick nod and said, "Thank you. Now, want to stick with thirteen, Crystelle?"

"That's my favorite number," Crystelle continued looking at the pad.

"Too big," Tara cut in again, "I'm telling you it's too big a number."

"Ya'll are so silly," Shelley stopped braiding, "I've been doing this stuff longer than any of you. If that's her number, then that's the number you use. It doesn't matter how big it is. Go on, Michelle." Shelley's head shook, as if she felt a tremendous shiver, and she took out the cornrow she had just finished and then started braiding it again.

"All right," Michelle whirled the marker in the air like a baton and tapped it against the pad. "Now I'm supposed to ask you to name four boys you like."

"Like how?" Crystelle asked.

"Look," Michelle said, "you want to find out who's going to like you, don't you?"

"Did I say that?"

"Yes, you did," Tara answered.

"Did I say that, Shelley?"

"Girl, name four of your little old boy friends and come on with this. When your hair is done, I'm going back in the house whether you're finished or not."

"Boyfriends? I don't have any boyfriends!"

"A boy friend, Crystelle, not a boyfriend. A boy that is your friend," Shelley responded.

"You have boys as friends, don't you?" Tara cut in.

"Yes she does."

"All right, then."

"If you had a boyfriend, we'd be doing a different one—so we know you don't have a boyfriend," Michelle explained.

"But you do have boys as friends," Tara repeated.

"So name them—four of them." Shelley was laughing with the other two by now.

"I don't think she's ready for this." Michelle put her marker down and looked to Tara for counsel.

"If she has to ask—"

"Oh, please, not that again. Okay, Willie, James, Byron, and—"

"I got it," Michelle interrupted Crystelle, "Byron and Jimmie."

"How did you know I was going to say Jimmie?"

Michelle looked up and looked back at the pad without saying a word. "Next question," she said with an exaggerated sigh. "Name four cities you want to live in."

"Oh, that's easy, Chicago, New York, Atlanta, and, I guess, Hollywood."

"Hollywood?" Tara shifted her upper body back before speaking again, whatchu wanna live way out there for?"

"Uh uh, girl, California is all that. That's where I'm gonna live, once I become a big singing sensation." Michelle pushed her fingertips against Crystelle's elbow. "We can be neighbors and walk our children through the hills together."

"What hills?" Crystelle asked.

"Oh, they got lots of hills out in Hollywood," Michelle continued writing in the names of cities as she spoke.

"Yeah, and lots of earthquakes, too," Shelley mentioned as she fixed another bead in Crystelle's hair.

"Earthquakes?" Michelle looked up at Shelley. She looked down at the pad at the last letters formed. "Looks like you may end up walking your baby with someone else."

"Please," Tara laughed, "You won't be going anywhere if you depend on your singing voice to carry you. Earthquakes don't have nothing to do with that one, honey."

"If anything," Shelley said, "you'll scare the earthquakes away. Or make them come."

"That's why I'm not gonna mention your names when I accept my Grammy." Michelle picked a scab on her knee as she spoke.

"That's why I'm not gonna say anything about your fantasizing to your Granny," Crystelle said.

Everyone looked at Crystelle. "Oooo," Tara said, "that was a corny one. Back to the thing."

"For real," Michelle waved and tapped the marker again, "how many kids you want, cornball?"

"Three."

"And if you don't get three?"

"Two."

"And if you don't get two?"

"Four."

"And if you don't get four?"

"Six."

"OK, now name four kinds of houses you might want to live in."

"Brick, condo, mansion, and castle." Crystelle felt the right side of her head. Shelley pushed her hand away.

"It's not ready for you to touch yet," Shelley explained.

Michelle bent over the pad and began moving the magic marker from word to word, assigning each a number. She reached the thirteenth, crossed it, and began again with one, counting until she reached thirteen a second time and crossed a new word. The pen moved with a silent beat, and Tara watched for a while. Shelley prepared to thread Crystelle's remaining strands of hair together. She gently pushed Crystelle's head to the left, and Crystelle looked up at the evening's rainbow.

Nighttime blue tiptoed in from a corner of sky to her right. She knew this even without looking, because she had seen skies like this before. The air felt warm, but it was almost autumn, and once white puffs of kept rain were stretched out and blushing. Rose and pink and purple floated in blue, and Crystelle knew that almost black approached from the right.

Crystelle thought about Tara's party two Saturdays ago. She had sat with Jimmie on the couch, watching Tara's father clear everybody out of his basement. Perspiration had sealed her blouse against her skin and taken the pressing out of her hair, sent it right back to how it looked before Shelley had put a hot comb to it earlier that day. She had felt excited, yet tired. The party had ended, but the red light still glowed. That's how the sky looked. Tired but happy from a daylong party. Shelley put the last bead in Crystelle's hair.

"Aren't you finished yet, Michelle?" Shelley asked, as she pressed and rubbed and pulled at Crystelle's hair with both hands.

"How'd you know?" Michelle held the pad up in front of herself and cleared her throat. Tara leaned back against her elbows and stretched her legs out. Crystelle felt her hair along with Shelley.

"I know 'cause I saw you put the marker down," Shelley replied.

"Ah hem," Michelle cleared her throat and straightened her back. She opened her mouth to speak, then looked up at Crystelle to make sure she was paying attention.

Michelle looked back at the pad and cleared her throat again. Then she said, "You're going to live in New York. You're going to have six kids."

"Six?" Shelley thrust her head forward.

Tara agreed with Shelley, "Girl, you ain't never gonna enjoy yourself with six whole kids."

"That's all right though, 'cause my girl is gonna live in a mansion!" Michelle's neck and head moved to the rhythm of her words.

"Yes, I will be visiting!" Tara threw her hand in the air and kicked her leg up.

Crystelle tapped her forefinger against her temple. "A mansion in New York."

Shelley smiled, "You're gonna need a mansion with seven kids."

"Six kids," Michelle corrected.

"And Jimmie makes seven, honey," Shelley leaned back on her elbows, arched her neck and head.

Crystelle stood up on her tiptoes and reached up to the sky.

"Now, you see now, that's the problem." Michelle was looking down at her pad and tapping it with her marker.

"What's the problem?" Shelley moved the top of her body toward Michelle. Crystelle's hands dropped to her sides and she leaned, flat-footed, against the steel rail banister.

"She isn't marrying Jimmie." Michelle kept her head still but blinked her eyes to catch everyone's reaction.

"Who's she going to marry?" Tara asked.

"Willy."

"That fool?" Tara asked.

Shelley looked up at Crystelle and said, "Quiet, Tara."

Crystelle looked down at Shelley and then down at the pad.

"You sure you counted right?" Shelley asked.

"Am I sure I counted right? Would I have done this thing if I thought I might not do it right? Don't blame me cause Jimmie's name got crossed out. I didn't tell her what number to pick."

"I told you it was too big from the get-go," Tara offered Crystelle.

"There isn't anything wrong with the number she picked." Michelle put her hands on her thighs and leaned toward Tara as she spoke. "Jimmie just isn't the one."

The girls sat and thought for a while. Crystelle heard the Western sky on the other side of the earth as it sucked up the last bit of her sun. Moths felt the transition to night and fled to the artificial haze of street lamps.

"Why do you think those stupid bugs fly around the lights every night?" Shelley asked.

"Trying to keep warm takes effort," Michelle offered.

"They're not trying to keep warm. It's eighty some degrees out here," Tara said. "They want to be where they can see everything."

"Now what's a moth gonna want to see?" Shelley asked. "That's where they plan to meet every morning before they go to bed. It's kind of like their little moth hang out."

"No," Crystelle said, "they miss the sun."

"So, you think they think the streetlight is the sun?" Shelley asked.

"They're a little sad but not stupid," Crystelle returned. "They know the light isn't a real sun. But they still keep on, flying around and around the next best thing to the real deal. It makes them feel better. They bump into the light and bounce back and then fly right on back into it. Or they fly into one another and fall a little. But then they fly right back up to that light and start flying around it again. They'd rather be around that lamp bumping into it and one another than be in the dark and alone." Crystelle shrugged her shoulders. "Beats a blank."

The four girls sat a little while longer and studied the flight patterns of moths around a not quite sun.

"That's what my Mamma told me, anyway."

Shelley pushed herself up and stretched. "Well, I can smell my dinner, and that's my signal to go in."

"Oh no, what time is it?" Crystelle jumped forward a little.

"I guess around nine." Michelle handed the magic marker up to Shelley as she spoke.

"I'll see ya'll later." Crystelle picked up her comb and threw her hand in farewell as she marched down the steps.

"Here, girl." Shelley ripped out the freshly marked page, walked down a few steps, and reached over the neighbor's bush to hand it to Crystelle. She smiled. Crystelle took the page without looking at it and smiled back. "Thanks for doing my hair for me, Shelley. You gonna braid it for me again next time?"

"Just make sure you tell me ahead of time if you're going to be all tender headed."

"All right," Crystelle laughed, "see ya."

Shelley called after her, "Remember not to wear any cotton scarves. They're the kind that dry your hair out."

Crystelle turned around to throw her hand up as Shelley walked into the house. Tara and Michelle waved back, and as Crystelle made her way down the street and climbed her own steps, she could still hear them talking on.

"Hollywood has too many earthquakes anyway. New York'll be just fine. I wouldn't want to live in nobody's Hollywood."

"What about your singing career?"

"Guess I'll just have to move to New York too."

"Honey, New York isn't any different from here. Believe me."

"How do you know?"

"I've been there."

"Really?"

The screen door slammed, and her mother's voice took over. "Crystelle!"

"Hey, mom! Whatchu doing? You eat yet?" Crystelle heard the splash of faucet water in a half-filled tub. She climbed the steps to the bathroom. Crystelle opened the door enough to poke her head in. Her mother lay in a soft pile of bubbles. "Whatcha doing? You eat yet?"

"What time is it, Crystelle?"

"I'm not sure."

"Are you sure it's past eight?"

"Pretty sure. You eat yet, Mommy?"

"So much for us enjoying a nice dinner together. Your grandfather is fast asleep and I'm on my way."

"You save me any?"

"Now what do you think? There's a plate on top of the stove."

"Mommy, why didn't you call me in for dinner?"

"Girl, at 8:00 you were spitting sunflower seeds out of your mouth."

"How'd you know that?"

"How did the whole block know is what you want to ask."

Crystelle walked in, plopped the toilet seat down, and sat as her mother spoke.

"And, Crystelle, please inform one Miss Michelle that she can not sing. Now, tell me something, why do ya'll have to be the loudest ones all the time?"

Crystelle stretched her legs out and leaned back.

"Once those boys left I couldn't hear anyone but you. Please try to remember people still have their windows open, now. Try to show some respect." Crystelle's mother propped herself up a little in the tub. "Your hair looks good."

"Oh, do you like it, Ma, really?"

"Yeah. Shelley can twist some head around, can't she?"

"Yeah."

"You hungry?"

"Yeah."

"I made pork chops. You're going to have to warm them up in the oven. Put them in—"

"I know, I know. Put them in one of the little tin pans."

"Sprinkle a little water in, to keep them from getting all dry."

"Okay, Ma." Crystelle tapped her left foot a few times.

"Don't get impatient, do you hear?"

"Yes."

"All right." She began rubbing soap in her washcloth. "So who ended up doing your little boy test?"

"Dag, you know everything."

"Shoot, I turned up the TV so I wouldn't have to hear Tara and Michelle. Don't nobody want to hear all that on their day off."

"Did Granddaddy hear it?"

"He fell asleep to it."

"Oh. Michelle did the whole thing."

"Oh."

"Who do you think I'm gonna marry, Mamma?"

"Nobody until you finish high school and college."

"Come on, Mom."

"Come on where?" She began moving the washcloth over her face and arms.

"Did you think you were gonna marry Daddy?"

"I knew it the minute I saw him." She splashed water over her face.

Crystelle watched the water roll down her mother's nose, her cheekbones, the lift in her chin.

"But, Crystelle, let me tell you something. Life is like a car ride. A long car ride. So, what do you do? You pack some sandwiches and buy some soda, so you can keep rolling without having to stop. You get the car checked out, fill up the gas, you buy yourself a map. But, you're not driving the car, Crystelle. You're not even on the passenger side. You're just in the back seat, watching the scenery. As much as you get all ready for the ride, you can never drive. You're just sitting in the back seat, chomping on a chicken sandwich, asking are we there yet."

"Mm."

"Now get out of here so I can have some privacy, please."

"What if I want to stay?" Crystelle grinned.

"What if you want to what? Girl you better get on—" Then the phone rang.

"Oops, gotta go." Crystelle jumped up and ran downstairs before the next ring stopped.

"Crystelle!" her mother called.

"Hold on, Jimmie. Yes, Mom!"

"That Miss Michelle—she never could count anyway."

Crystelle smiled and got back on the telephone.

*   *   *   *

A lurch sent her face forward, away from the cradle of her hand. Crystelle looked out of the window into the darkness, then up into the brown brown of the old train conductor. It was now again.

"Get your things, Little Lady," he smiled. "Philly's next."

Crystelle smiled back and thanked the man for remembering her.

"Had yourself a little dream there, didn't ya?"

Crystelle looked up from her lap and back into the train conductor's face. His hat was cocked a little to the side and he rested one hand on the seat in front of Crystelle's as the train hit a slow curve. "Yeah, I guess I was dreaming a little. Why?

Did I talk in my sleep or something?" Crystelle sent a little giggle out after her question.

"You could say something like that."

"Whatchu mean?" Crystelle smiled in his face again.

"Naw. You know. The train's empty this time a night. Don't nobody really get on at the few places we stop. So I was sittin' just over there, you know." The conductor pointed a few rows up and across from Crystelle's seat.

"So, was I talking out loud in my sleep?"

"Naw, not really." The man looked at his watch.

"Well, how did you know I was—"

"Naw, you know, you just shook around a lot."

"I did?"

"Yeah, you know, like you sleep wild. But then you did mumble something . . . I wasn't listening or nothin' . . . I just heard you mumble somethin' . . . and I said to myself, naw, she ain't no wild sleeper, she's just dreaming."

"Oh, was I all loud and stuff?" Crystelle put her hand, cupped, in front of her mouth.

"Naw, it wasn't bad. I just could hear you a little, you know." He looked back at his watch again. "I was gonna wake you up a little sooner, though." He kind of looked away but at Crystelle's face at the same time.

"How come?"

"I dunno. It's none of my business, you know."

"Yeah?" Crystelle blinked and waited.

"I'm saying."

Crystelle just waited. She wanted to say yeah again, but she just waited.

"You just tossed and turned, you know. Seemed kinda uncomfortable, that's all. Was you . . . were you dreaming about running or falling or something like that?"

"No. I was just sitting mostly in my dream. I was just dreaming about home."

"Oh, you mean a dream you keep having?" The man looked away from Crystelle and at his wristwatch while she nodded. An image of this man, reaching into his pocket to pull out a gold timepiece, flashed, then flashed away.

"Yeah. It was a dream I have about home."

"You visiting family?"

"Yes, I'm going home."

"That's good," he said, as he walked away. "No matter how far you roam, sure enough you got to get back home." He walked to the doorway behind Crystelle as the train pulled in along the platform.

Crystelle stood with her bag.

"You have a nice visit now, Miss."

"Thank you. Thank you for waking me up in time."

"No problem." He stepped out first and then extended his hand for Crystelle to step down off the train. "Don't worry, Little Lady," the older man said, as he turned to walk up along the length of the sitting train, "you'll be fine."

Crystelle stood there watching the conductor walk away. The other exiting passengers sort of swept her up in the direction of the stairwell out of the tunnel. Crystelle looked at the man one more time and smiled at his back before she walked away.

She walked up the steps into the Thirtieth Street station and headed toward the taxi stand. The high ceilings carried a sound like flight, and Crystelle looked up to see a pigeon flying past a row of stained-glass windows. She wondered how the trapped pigeons find their way out, if they ever escaped, as she left the old building. She jumped into the first cab parked out front and told him the way she wanted him to drive.

"Miss, it'll be faster if I head this way."

Crystelle saw him point toward Center City as she watched his face in his rear view mirror.

"I want the scenic route," she insisted and looked at him until he looked away.

As the car swerved along the Schukhill River, Crystelle gazed out at the lighted boathouses on the other side. Out across the gray blue of the expressway, the dark blue, the almost black, of the river, loomed the boathouses, each frame lined with strings of bulbs. Their white lights cut the night. When the cab whizzed past them, everything on the other side of the river fell back to black.

The meter's click and the muffler's hum filled space in the moving car. Crystelle tried to take herself back to her dream. What did he say on the phone? She went back to that night. What did he say? Crystelle couldn't remember. She stopped trying and let the taxi race her back to West Philly. The wide lawns along City Line Avenue's hotels and restaurants gave way to row houses almost as soon as the cab turned by the Adam's Mark hotel. They drove past the park, under the el for a minute, then turned onto Frazier Street. A few streetlights flickered in the dark. The street was like a Christmas tree—it looked narrower and narrower to her each year.

Granddaddy stood at the top of the stoop as Crystelle climbed out of the cab.

"You got money for the hack?"

"Sure, Granddaddy."

"You paid him?"

"Yeah." Crystelle breathed the sweet body oil Granddaddy still wore and felt the strong love in his weak arms. He reached for the bag, but Crystelle swung it into the house ahead of him. She watched him turn to lock the doors.

"You sure you got money for the hack?"

"Yeah, Granddaddy, it's done. I got money."

"Good, 'cause I ain't got none."

"Crystelle, baby!" Mamma came down the steps in house slippers and sweats.

"Mamma, baby!"

Soon Crystelle had thrown on an old pair of her college sweatpants too. She ate some leftovers saved just for her and watched a little TV with her family.

"All these channels." Mamma clicked the remote. "Don't know what we're paying for."

"Told you not to get it." Granddaddy shifted on his old couch. "Don't need it."

"I can't get anything without cable."

"Get a VCR and a video card. What you need extra stations for? See what you want."

"You know you watch it. Here." Mamma gave up the remote.

Crystelle lay back and listened to the hum of voices stream through the room. She wanted to tell them both about the voices that were flowing to her each time she closed her eyes. She wanted to tell them that, even with her eyes shut tight, she saw them all, all of them, in a dance with time. That the thoughts were flowing to her, and she had no control over the dream shift. It just happened, so easy, every time she closed her eyes. She wanted to tell them both that sometimes she longed for the shift, that she wanted to shift away in time, and that she was sleeping more so that Jimmie could still dance with her spirit in time. She thought about telling them about last night. But it felt like now she just wanted to lay back and hear their voices. She could be in time now and hear her mamma and her grandfather and not have to think too much. It felt good to hear them like that. Then, Crystelle thought of Hamp, sort of, and she reached back for the telephone.

"Hey, what you punching in all those numbers for?"

"I'm using my calling card."

"I'm asking you who you calling long distance and you just got here."

"I just want to make sure Hamp knows where I am."

Mamma took a sip of her bubbly water. "Make sure?"

"I just had time to leave a message. I want to make sure."

"Make sure?"

"That he got it."

"He don't have this number?" Mamma took another sip.

"Hey!" Crystelle stood up and walked back into the house toward the living room.

"Cord don't stretch but so far," Mamma mumbled.

"Hey, baby, why'd you leave me?" Hamp whispered into the phone.

"I didn't leave you, honey." Crystelle glanced over at the couch, and the couch glared back at her.

"Are you all right?"

"Of course. I just decided to be home for a minute."

"Why?"

Crystelle listened to the sound of air beating through the telephone.

"Why, what made you want to go home all of a sudden?"

"I don't know."

"I'll come get you."

"Get me?"

"You don't have to ride the bus again."

"I took the train." Crystelle pulled the spiral cord, made it straight, watched it bounce back up to a spiral cord again.

"I'll drive you back."

"You really don't have to come all the way down here just to turn around."

"I could stay a night."

"Well . . ."

"That boy don't need to be comin' down here. This is family time." Crystelle turned her back more, but she couldn't block her granddaddy's voice. "Tell him you'll see him when you get back up."

"So what do you say, Crystelle?" Hamp's voice turned low. It was his serious voice, even on the telephone.

Crystelle cut Granddaddy a look that demanded quiet. Then she begged. Granddaddy's eyes crackled back. She could hear the volume on the TV rise when she turned back around to talk on the phone.

"Hey, baby."

"Glad to know somebody down there loves me."

"I love you." And she did. She loved him for the high-top fade that grew into locks that he cut one day with her. She loved him for not wanting to cut his locks but doing it because he had to. She loved him for loving her. How could she not love him? He was still loving her. So she did too.

"So, you want me to drive down Sunday?" His soul reached out to her, breathing deeply, and she felt his embrace in the sound of air in and out through full man's lips.

"MmHm."

"Huh?"

"No. No, baby."

"No what?"

"Hold on." Crystelle kept the phone to her ear but moved the mouthpiece away from her face, then up again. She could hear him breathe out. "Baby, I'll see you when I get back up there."

"'Cause it's family time."

"Kinda." Crystelle looked deep into the dark kitchen, just through the living room and the dining room.

"Thought I was part of it."

"Mm." She looked down.

"You want to make a family?"

"Yeah." She looked up again.

"Then what's the problem? You can't be Daddy's little girl and my baby too. Hello? This is too much. I can't even pick my own woman up. I said hello. Who're you hiding?"

"MmMm." Crystelle pulled the cord and watched it bounce back up, and again, and then she pulled and watched it bounce one more time.

"So you can't talk straight when you're home? Hello?"

"Dag, Hamp, I'm here."

"I'm out."

"Huh?"

"Huh. Huh. That's all you got to say? I'm out. Peace."

"You gonna call me tomorrow?" Crystelle couldn't feel the beat of air through phone any more.

"Nah. Hello?"

"No?"

"Nah. It's your family time. I'm out. All right?"

"You gonna call me tomorrow?"

"Nah. I'm out."

"You not gonna call me?"

"I'll talk to you later."

"Tomorrow?"

"Nah, baby. Chill with your family. I'm gonna chill up here."

"You gonna chill?"

"You heard me, Crystelle."

"I'll talk to you tomorrow."

"Oh yeah? I hope I'm home when you call."

"Call me early. Everybody gets up early." Crystelle needed to hear the beat. His breath reaching out to hers, even on the telephone. She needed to hear it again.

"I'm not calling you, baby. I'll speak to you later on . . . Hello?"

"You my man?"

"Why do you keep getting all quiet on the long distance?"

"I'm thinking."

"Oh yeah?"

"Yeah. What time are you calling?"

"Naw——"

"Hamp."

"What you think——"

"Are you my man? What are you laughing at?"

"You."

"Are you my man?"

"Yeah——"

"Then you need to be calling me." He didn't answer. Crystelle was about to say hello herself, but she didn't. She just listened for the breathing sound to come through the telephone again. She was just listening.

"I'll speak to you later," he said.

"Yeah?"

"Yeah," Hamp sent out air like he had been running hard for a minute or two. "Yeah. All right." He breathed in again.

She heard it. She heard him breathe again. It wasn't the lovelove breath pouring from his soul, but it was something. She would have to say something.

"I'ma feel you tonight, honey." Crystelle leaned over and whispered.

"Yeah?"

"Yeah."

She shifted back to her normal voice. "I'll speak to you later."

"MmHm."

Crystelle looked around when she hung up the telephone. Her mother was sitting on the old, green sofa next to Granddaddy.

"I'm saying this," Mamma said without looking away from the TV. "Don't be beggin' no man to call here no more."

"We just have some things to work out."

"MmHm."

"It's all good, Mamma. Really. We're fine. We just gotta—"

"Work it out?"

"Yeah."

"All I'm saying is him callin' you shouldn't be one of them."

Crystelle squeezed in between Mamma and Granddaddy on the couch. "Mamma baby." Crystelle put her head on her mamma's shoulder like a little girl. Then she lifted her head, kissed Granddaddy on the cheek, and put her head back down.

"He's your boyfriend?" Mamma shrugged her left shoulder up and turned to look in Crystelle's face. "You don't think you deserve a man that's gonna give you space?"

"Mamma, it's not about all that."

"Yes it is."

"Sometimes you have to—"

"Crystelle, please, it's that man's job to call."

Granddaddy turned the volume back down.

Crystelle lay back on the couch without speaking and half-watched the stations turn with her family. She could half-hear her mother rise and climb the creaky stairs for bed. In the dark of the closed-in porch, Crystelle let her body take up all the space Granddaddy's body left over. His breathing became stronger and even. She knew he wouldn't make it as far as his bed. Black-and-white reruns rolled on the new color TV. The past was playing now, but Granddaddy was sleeping through what had been his present. *The Honeymooners* played and played on.

She pulled a clean blanket over her mother's father and, turning the TV off, climbed the creaky stairs herself. Mamma had laid out one of her own nightgowns. Crystelle stripped and dressed and lay back. The breeze blowing through her window brought in outside smells. Hamp floated into her mind, but he didn't stay. He drifted away. She rolled over onto her arm and kissed it. She just gave herself a quick kiss, smiled, and thought about practicing kissing when she was younger in that very same space. She tasted Mamma's cocoa butter smell when she kissed herself. She rolled over again and looked down at the dresser drawer. She knew there was a Ziploc bag there. She could see it even without getting out of the bed to look. Sleep didn't come, but something else did, a remembrance.

Crystelle remembered a moment in a moment one year. It felt like something was over and maybe something else was beginning, but then again, maybe not.

The smell of flowers filled the air. Full bloom wafting from here to everywhere. Scent filled her head and hair and clothes. Cut flowers filled the house and bees and early-on mosquitoes followed their sweet trail and hummed about in rhythm. May was falling into garbage cans and dirt yards and sewer drains. Spring never seems to last long, she thought. The first part still feels cold and the last part feels hot and you've got this little slice of time in between that could honestly be called springlike and comfortable.

And so the sweet smell danced around with the rain smell on Frazier Street. Mamma and Crystelle put on their best white. Mamma had starched and ironed and starched and ironed and cried a little, too, so that now when Crystelle got dressed, the sweet smell and the rain smell and a starch smell floated up to her collar and darted into all her senses. Mamma hadn't ironed for her in years.

Crystelle thought it had been natural for one of the nappyheads to start throwing flowers at her dancing feet as she slid under the ropes and double-dutched to the rhythm of girl-time song. And who but Jimmie Johnson would be the first to exchange pebbles for sweets to aim at her slip-slap feet? How was she to know that, before she could even get used to flowers from Jimmie Johnson, so many hands would slip fresh arrangements in their place? Not for her, but for him.

So, she had sat on Granddaddy's couch in her starched white with her hands folded and a Ziploc bag full of dried-out petals in her bottom dresser drawer. She sent no flowers to Jimmie, though. She knew he wouldn't make use of them. She sent some in his mother's name but not in Jimmie's. Crystelle had given him a dandelion once in time long passed, but she had never asked Jimmie if boys kept Ziploc bags in their dresser drawers.

So she sat and she cried and she waited. Mamma didn't say much to her now, because Jimmie's gone was for good without a bit of goodness. So what could Mamma say?

The rain stopped and it looked bright bright out the porch window. The sky light blue and sunbeams bouncing about in all that blue, reflecting the blue back onto earth.

Crystelle and her mamma and her granddaddy walked the two corners it took to get to the parlor that day. Jimmie's uncle would drive them to the graveyard later. They were early but the room filled up fast. Guess everyone thought they were close enough to get there quick.

The sweet smell mixed with sweat as she entered the parlor and took her seat. All of Frazier Street and most of springtime West Philly were on their way.

She was surrounded by the love and the loneliness. The whispers and wails were like wind in her ears she could hear but couldn't understand. A fan turned overhead. It carried the sounds from all around the room. Sucked in sound and sent it out again softly.

It was too close and it was too much. Arms pulled her close, shaking or patting as if she were a burping child. Hot breath, moist like fog, rolled down her neck. Faces wet along cheeks and over the whispers and cries rubbed against her starched white collar. Crystelle felt it go limp. The white white was turning rouge. All the loving in the parlor could only pull Crystelle back from alone. It couldn't push her out of lonely. Along her smiles salty wet would slide, going down.

Through the crush of flesh and dim of tears she could see the only flowers a boy had ever given her, and the emptiness in the sweet air that meant he was gone. Crystelle's row rose and strained necks and looked at Jimmie gone. No one rushed her, and she leaned forward to whisper a poem in Jimmie's dead ear. Now that all the closest friends and family had taken their last look at the body, the Reverend spoke on and on about the soul.

Crystelle heard the women crying. Their cries were long and high. In the sobbing song of the women she felt her spirit rise out of her self. Her spirit could feel the feeling behind each song. Each voice, each spirit.

She looked back at the girls her age, the ones who knew Jimmie and the ones who really didn't. Her spirit floated out and met theirs, and they danced to the sobbing song. In the dance she could feel more. Girls who didn't know Jimmie were sobbing because they never would. Girls who'd known Jimmie were sobbing because they didn't know enough. They were dancing and singing a spirit dance and song because they knew Crystelle's loss was their loss too. They knew. They were tired and a little old now. It was enough. None of them wanted anymore. It was time for it all to end.

Crystelle looked back at Jimmie. She felt her spirit dance with his in time. The pop and the snap hurled her spirit further. The pop in Jimmie's body and the snap in her own. She remembered. She felt her spirit go back to his the moments he began to pass. She felt him back to just before the passage, to almost after living. First she felt the anger, the confusion, and then she felt herself. She felt his spirit clutching hers now back on that street. Felt his sobs fall out into her soul. They fell out in tears, so quiet. There was more.

She could feel the tremors that forced his body to shake and sweat and sob inside. The tremors passed through his body and, in the place where they could meet beyond time, his tremors entered her. His sobs were hers, deep and silent and whole-body shaking.

Crystelle could see clearly. She wasn't even at the funeral parlor anymore. The street was black, but above Jimmie's deeply sobbing body, the light was strong. She could see Jimmie's blood seep into the cracks along Frazier Street. It seemed his blood was filling all the cracks in the dark. She rushed to stop the flow. With her hands she tried. She tried to use her shirt, to rip off a part of her blouse to cover the place the blood was flowing out of. She needed to cover the hole a boy still standing right there had made in Jimmie. Arms tried to pull her back but she threw her own body over his and held on tight. That close. She looked into his eyes big and bright from seeing too much now. Oh, Jimmie she cried out loud. But it was only a whisper. With the crying whisper she tasted his breath in her mouth and knew he tasted hers too. So close. They could exchange the taste of breath like that. It frightened her, and she closed her own lips tight.

The light above them was strong. She peered into him as he fixed his eyes, saw his own decision to die. She could see it was a choice. He was bearing witness right before her eyes, looking into a time she couldn't see. His eyes shined bright bright, like mirrors reflecting herself back onto herself. She watched her face, contorted and weird in his reflective bright bright eyes now. She locked on the look of herself distorted, but Jimmie was catching a glimpse of the eternal. She felt that glance into all time make the final tremor easier for him. A tear fell and followed his down the brown smooth of his face. She watched her tear chasing his; and then, when she looked up into his eyes again, they were shut tight. Then she could breathe in. And out.

As her spirit flew back in time now, she saw what had been unseeable that night. The circle of light from the strong street lamp above, and Jimmie stretched out long and full. And herself. She could see herself mourning, crouched low and tight. She was crumpled over him, and the tremors were all hers now.

Deep tonal sounds hurled out from the space where she crouched on Frazier Street. Like a ring. A deep bong of sound reverberated. But it didn't come from her, or from the blood-stained street where Crystelle crouched and wailed. The rich wave of ringing sound came from an outline of Jimmie, a shape of his eighteen flesh years now caught in an image of brown light and vibrating song. The pop and the snap had dispirited them both. The outline of Crystelle, snapped out of her seventeen years of flesh, looked up, sounded a response ring light and high, saw the light above Jimmie, and eased back into Crystelle.

But the spirit of Jimmie flew forward instead of up and away, reached out to Crystelle's spirit, and pulled.

Just as Mamma and Granddaddy were pulling on Crystelle's back and shoulders, crouched low, Jimmie's spirit yanked too. He pulled on her very soul. Crystelle felt herself being emptied out, hollowed, and shrieked. The streetlight crackled darkness against this new sound and shattered into the hot night air above Frazier Street.

Crystelle had never seen that before. She started to shake the memories away, turned over on her bed.

She came back to the funeral home, circled the air, winding

among the whiring fans, then left that memory, too, and followed the cocoa butter smell.

Crystelle simply wasn't ready for the loneliness. The loneliness that crept into her life after that. Like the seasons. Like a routine. A ritual where she felt sacrificed, even though he was gone. A gone gone.

And it seemed no one felt the loneliness. And it seemed no one understood the loneliness. And it seemed it would always be her loneliness.

She felt it so deep inside, she could feel her spirit cry out softly. And, she couldn't cry. She had to be so strong. Every one was so strong she had to be so strong only inside could she feel her spirit only her spirit could inside her cry out softly in the night in the day like seasons like moons like a spin like one spin and she could feel the soft cry.

And she had to let go. And she could not let go.

All she had was the feeling that, like a father, he'd return.

Crystelle turned over, closed her eyes, kissed the cocoa butter smell. She tasted the cocoa butter one last time before she turned over again, facing the dresser, and fell asleep. Her spirit would have to flex backward, dance in time, float and shift through the eye only her mind could use to see. One more time.

Chapter Three

The house was quiet enough for Crystelle to know Mamma was at work and Granddaddy was out too. It sounded like afternoon. Crystelle heard a ringing in her ears. Aunt Brenda was calling. She'd heard Crystelle was in town and, of course, she had to come on over and be home, be in her second home. In Jimmie's home.

When she hung up with Brenda Johnson, she decided to wash up and cross over right away. Aunt Brenda wasn't just Jimmie's mother. She was also one of her own mother's closest friends. Besides that, visiting her Aunt Brenda was one of the things Crystelle figured she had come home to do.

The time came to climb the stairs across the street. Crystelle could feel herself walking, and she could hear the echoes of double-dutch song. Off in the distance a little boy danced, and Crystelle could see him dancing there. Her Aunt Brenda saw Crystelle seeing the little boy. She could see Crystelle, stuck there in the middle of Frazier Street.

She had to find a way to get across. Crystelle heard the screen door open loud and high. Then she heard it slam. But to his own beat the little boy danced so far away, and Crystelle didn't want to stop seeing him dancing there. It was nice to be on Frazier Street and look up just like that while walking across the street to Aunt Brenda's house and there, just so easy, see a boy dancing. The bassline thumped out of someone's bedroom window and into Crystelle's spirit. She emptied out and felt her essential self dancing to the deep rhythms echoing down Frazier Street. Her spirit danced with the little boy, old school style, happy, even though he was up the street, away, dancing in front of his own friends. They danced together, even though he thought he was all alone in the middle of Frazier Street. She saw an outline of herself, so far away.

Aunt Brenda walked down and out and hugged Crystelle close, then held her back, each middle finger almost touching each thumb around Crystelle's upper arms. Crystelle looked in her eyes and smiled. Brenda could see her own child reflected there, but she'd expected that.

Crystelle was looking off again but Aunt Brenda had her arm around her now and she was walking. Aunt Brenda led her up the stoop. The screen door creaked and fell back softly this time. The living room was hot and dark. Plastic hissed after Crystelle sat down. Then, it was quiet.

"Well, Lil' Crystelle, girl, how you been?" Aunt Brenda's plastic slipcover didn't make a hissing sound.

"Oh fine, Aunt Brenda."

"Girl, I haven't seen you since two Christmases ago."

"That's right," Crystelle counted backward in her head.

"I was so proud of you, coming home from Penn State."

"MmHm." The sofa hissed as Crystelle sat back.

"And here you are now, all college graduated and all. Working a good job. Well, we all knew you were going to do well, leaving high school with honors."

"You remember?" she kept counting back.

"Of course I do. After watching you grow up, I felt like I was graduating again."

"Mmm." She wanted to stop counting. Time didn't want to roll back a whole lot more.

"You had something to eat yet?"

"Not yet."

"Let's fix a little something together. We never did that before. I've got some chicken seasoned in the kitchen." Both women stood up, and the plastic slipcover hummed a last time.

Brenda's house was shaped just like Crystelle's mamma's. If the porch lasted for a minute, the living room took up forty-three seconds. In a blink you easily missed the dining room, but then you stepped into the kitchen. The kitchen lay vast as the sea compared to all the puddles a person had to skip over to get there. It was big, and the back door led to the most yard you could ever expect out of a West Philly alley. Upstairs, Crystelle knew, Brenda and James's bedroom looked out front. Past the bathroom another bedroom looked out the back, and a den sort of squeezed in the middle. The other bedroom was Jimmie's, and Crystelle wondered without asking if Brenda had changed it around too.

"Aunt Brenda, what'd you do with that big ol' orange painting that used to be hanging there?"

"Girl, first I tried to sell it but found I couldn't give it away. If there is a garbage man like Roc working the streets of West Philly, his wife is probably hating me right now for putting it on the street."

"What about the zodiac poster?"

"Same street, same day."

"And all the old furniture?"

"The used furniture man hauled it——"

"——same day?"

"Yeah, honey. One day I just decided to clear everything out. The next day it was all gone. Rooms were all bare down here. But I liked it. Kept it that way for a while. Took my time painting. Buying a little piece here. A little piece there."

"I know your husband was losing his patience with you."

"No, not really." Brenda turned to start walking back to the kitchen again. "He was going through his own thing around that time."

Crystelle followed Brenda through the tiny dining room with her eyes cast down. She could see four valleys in the carpet where the big wooden table once stood. The big table Aunt Brenda used to polish every week. That the Johnsons only set for holidays.

"I had been saving all along for Jimmie to go to college too."

Crystelle looked up into chrome, along the small glass tabletop, and into the kitchen. 'Someday,' Aunt Brenda used to say, 'I'm gonna set this thing for all my grandchildren.' Then she would smile and look at Crystelle, even if her eyes were looking the other way.

But Aunt Brenda was talking right now. "After a while, I figured I might as well use that little bit of money, so I fixed up the house."

Crystelle tapped the glass table and pointed her toes so the top of her shoe pressed into the space where massive wood had stood for almost twenty years. Almost all their lives. With the glass table that only sat four, Brenda's dining room felt huge, airy, almost fresh. Crystelle followed her into the kitchen and sat on one of the new barstools. Brenda handed her an onion, so Crystelle slowly started to peel away each outer layer. She felt the brown skin, like paper, flake and fall out of her fingers.

While Crystelle chopped, Brenda lit the stove, threw the meat in a pan, chopped a pepper. She poured iced tea into thick glasses and put the glasses into the freezer. She pulled out the plates and poured beans and rice into a deep pot to heat up and then cool. One tear fell out of Crystelle's stinging eyes.

Crystelle could sit where she was and see everything. The back door open to the yard, the cupboard open to the shelves, the oven door open to darkness. Crystelle could look into everything because Brenda had everything open wide, from the clothes dryer to the ice box. Brenda took her time closing a door once she'd opened it up. So, Crystelle looked around. She saw what she saw. And she listened close because she heard everything her best friend's mother was telling her. Crystelle could tell that if this was what she wanted to do, then this was what she had to do.

"It took a while."

"It did?"

"Deciding to do this or the other. It was something I hadn't thought of getting done because I never thought I'd be able to. At least, not any time soon. But, then, I took a look around. It was just after the time I had taken for myself . . . you know."

"Yes."

"And I remember the day, Crystelle Clear. It was clear and bright and trying to get cold outside. You had gone off on your first year at the college, and it felt so—ya'll used to make so much noise," Brenda laughed.

"We weren't that bad."

"Oh yes ya'll were. The whole block kept track of Frazier Street without going near a window. Just hearing ya'll all day. Your friends and his friends too. Loud, crazy children. Happy. Well, that fall just slipped on down so quiet on me, Crystelle. Too quiet. But not bad quiet. Just, a change. So, I said, I might as well go all the way."

"Just change everything."

"Yeah, girl."

"What did Uncle James say?"

"I'm telling you, I never even discussed it with him."

"You just started taking out all that money?"

"Wasn't the money he missed so much as the changes in the house. Every day he would come home to something new." Brenda set the plates down and took a sip of her glass. "First, everything down here was gone. At once. And I mean every-thing. All gone."

Crystelle silently remembered her junior prom picture with Jimmie still next to a couple of his baby pictures in the front room.

"Then, little by little, new stuff just kept coming in."

"And he never even brought it up?"

"Not at first. I mean, after he figured out we hadn't been robbed." Brenda laughed and looked away for a second or two. "James never really did chill out here anyway. He likes to watch his TV up in the room, and he likes to eat his dinner in front of it."

"But Mamma and them used to be up in here all the time."

"Not so much as in the summer. Wintertime folks stay in more. And, truthfully, wasn't no one in here much even that summer. Didn't feel like partying that much then."

The women kept eating and talking. The doors were still open. The sun slowly fell through the farthest piece of sky.

"I mean, you know, he started making little jokes here and there. 'What you gon' do next, knock down a wall? Is this the right house? Is you the woman I married?' That's what he would say," Brenda changed her voice and then changed it again. "He'd say, like, 'My key is workin' and you look like my wife, but this don't look like the same place I woke up in and walked out of this morning.' And I'd say, 'James, you don't know me no more, baby?' And he'd say, 'I don't know. Man can't be too sure.' And I'd say, 'Come on over here, baby, and I'll show ya.'" Brenda smiled in her glass and then up at Crystelle. "And I did."

"Oh, Aunt Brenda."

"Honey, he knew I was his wife again."

"Aunt Brenda!"

"Shoot, girl, you grown now. I'm happy to be able to talk to you like a woman." She took a sip. "Yeah, we got it all back together about then, too. And then, well, I was finished. The house was done."

Brenda's face turned serious. "Always looked forward to the day I would look at you and see a woman grown and be able to talk to you woman-like." Brenda smiled again. "Yeah, honey, I'm glad you came home."

Brenda sat sipping her drink, while Crystelle cleared the table. She wiped the new table after she loaded the dishwasher.

"Whew, well," Brenda said standing up, "let's see what's so special about that room to that old husband of mine."

"You want to go upstairs?"

"Let's watch some TV."

Crystelle watched Aunt Brenda close the doors and followed her up the stairs.

They sat watching and not really laughing. Aunt Brenda spent a lot of time with the remote. Then a movie came on.

"Finally," Aunt Brenda said.

Crystelle lay down with a blanket tossed over her and her head resting on a pillow on Aunt Brenda's lap. Brenda pulled through Crystelle's hair, lulling her.

"I don't know why you decided to relax your hair, girl. I remember when you used to keep beads on your braids years ago. Could hear them clickin' every time you jumped double dutch outside. Could hear them click clickin' when you would come runnin' through the house. Your hair would strike a beat and let folks know: Crystelle Clear's in the house. Take notice." Aunt Brenda started all over again on the other side of Crystelle's hair, softly pulling. "Glad to see you, honey. Glad you're here in this room."

* * * *

Crystelle opened her eyes and then jumped a little without moving. The motionless jump was an inside jump, and Crystelle woke up all the way. The TV sat silent and the room was dark.

Crystelle was thirsty and she had to pee. She lay there longer, wishing she didn't have to pee. She could go back to sleep thirsty but not without going to the bathroom. Crystelle decided to get a quick drink first. Then she could slip back upstairs, pee, and sleep. Really all she wanted to do was sleep.

She tossed the blanket off and slid her feet into her sneakers. She stood at the doorway to the den and looked right into the dark of the second bedroom. Crystelle knew no one was sleeping there. She knew she didn't need to turn on more than the nightlight that was throwing a glow downstairs. She would return to the den soon.

The stairs creaked as she stepped down. Crystelle could just see her way through the first floor with the light of the streetlamps and the dull glow of the nightlights plugged in all around the house. She looked down to find her way, and there she could just catch the glass table shining like a skyscraper on ancient grounds. Crystelle could hear the spirits chant and cry, confused by images reflected in modern glass. She thought she could see herself in the glass and steel, too, distorted, like spirits on what had always been sacred earth, dancing in the too-bright light of sun reflected in forty-story twentieth century mirror.

A spirit sang here, too, just on the edge of the far valley in Aunt Brenda's rug. Crystelle did not strain to hear. Just like people rush in and out of the tall mirrored office building, thinking only of electric green ideas on black screens, she could see herself in the steel and glass of this small table her Aunt

Brenda bought with money she got because she could make the electric ideas blink and move behind the screen.

Crystelle could hear something, but she kept on, stepped into the kitchen, and clicked on the light. White noise crackled. Then, all she could hear was the refrigerator's hum and the far off sound of cats howling for love in the night.

Chapter Four

The next day sun was shining somewhere between summer and autumn, sometime between morning and afternoon. Sweat stuck shirt to skin. She pulled her leggings, felt the spandex pull little hairs on her skin. Her hand dug deep to scratch scalp. New growth lay thick and strong under a layer of straightened hair. She could feel the chemicals along the stiff outer layer. Aunt Brenda was right. The stuff on top wasn't real.

She stumbled into the bathroom, and, finally, sat down. The long stream trailed out of her body. She looked up and saw the bottle of Old Spice on the windowsill next to the sink. Uncle James always wore Old Spice. Crystelle washed her hands quick—didn't even bother to run some toothpaste in her mouth. She hurried back to the middle room. She was ready to go.

After she folded the blanket and arranged a few pillows, Crystelle leaned against the door and saw the way her own room fit into that space. She opened the door, skipped down the stairs, stopped, and walked into the kitchen.

Aunt Brenda sat with a bowl of cereal. "I slept late too, honey. How ya feel?"

"All right. Did I miss Uncle James?"

"Yeah. He's off to work 6:00 every day this week."

"You working at the hospital today?"

"Yeah, I hafta be in by two. You wanna get yourself something to eat?"

"No thanks. I'm gonna head home. See who called. Shower."

"Sounds like a winner."

"Thanks for letting me crash."

"Child, please, you're in your home."

Crystelle smiled and blew a kiss.

"That's right—don't try to put no funky two-day-old underarm around me."

"Yeah, yeah." Crystelle waved her hand, then turned and smiled again as she walked through the house. She stepped onto the stoop, checking the door behind her like habit.

"Sure didn't change those slam locks like everything else," Crystelle thought to herself. Many a time crazy Jimmie let it close behind him but ahead of his key. Then he would have to stay at her house until someone came home. Sometimes, Crystelle used to think, maybe he left his key inside on purpose.

Crystelle walked across the street. Hamp would leave it inside on purpose too. He had. That's why she was home. She felt her belly. The firm mound she rubbed. It felt bloated but firm. Tight or taught. One of those. No tests. No discussions. Just a feeling and a man who wanted a baby too badly and had left it in more than once.

Maybe her body would flow tonight. She looked up and knew the moon was there, even though she couldn't see it. The sun shined too brightly, too bright for the moon.

"Granddaddy!" Crystelle called as she jumped upstairs. She checked the answering machine in Mamma's room. No beeping light. "Granddaddy!" She was kicking off her sneakers when she saw her grandfather's scrawl taped to the banister. "Meet me at the free library."

In the silence of things around her, Crystelle could think through the men she loved now to the first man she had ever loved. Men without fathers search for models when young, look for ways to be men. Some remain in boyhood throughout their lives. Women without fathers search for models when older, search for mates. Some never find the best match throughout their lives. Jimmie had had his father, and Crystelle had her grandfather.

As Crystelle showered and dressed and walked along, she could see her Granddaddy now. Rubbing nickels, because he had worked since before children should be made to work and all that working had pushed him up to just making it. So he stood frail but strong, and each week he stood just like that and walked to the free library. He had started going since he had stopped looking. Since he saw as far as he could see and no more work was in sight. And he stopped thinking about going back down South. What good would he be in that place where all he'd known was twisting chicken heads and pushing mules? Since seventeen he'd stopped holding animals. Since his own father lost all the land and all the animals to a government loan, he'd learned the touch of cool machine in the morning turning hot where his hand lay by night.

Now his hand lay on books, and he sat, finally, in a room filled with words. There he read ben-Jochannan and Diop and Van Sertima. He read Baldwin and Ellison. Hurston and he learned about women. Now, at almost seventy, learning about women. He read Brent. Toomer and Larsen, Wright and Douglass. He read the Black paper and the white one. He'd read *The Black Scholar, The Journal of Negro Education*. He read *The Final Call*.

He sat with other men who couldn't find decent work. Men who couldn't see being a messenger, mailer, or cleaning man to white folk younger and less educated but who had college degrees. Men who had been too old to apply at the post office but too young to retire. Men who had been turned out. They'd meet and play chess and talk about first love in the South and last pain in the North. They'd talk these oldren. Talk about what they'd read. About Max Robinson and *Good Times*. About Randall Robinson and reparations. About liquor and Lourde. So, Crystelle's granddaddy knew the folk older and younger than him standing and talking to the streets. Drunk and sloppy on the corner, rambling to the world. He saw them and sometimes he even listened. He knew he was just a family's love away from standing there himself. He knew his daughter saved his life. It was something they could all know and not have to say.

"Hey, Granddaddy."

"Hey, Clear as Crystelle Girl."

"Mamma get out to work on time today?"

"Always do." Granddaddy looked up at Crystelle and smiled. He had the paper spread out before him.

Crystelle sat down on the long table scratched out with scrawl. It was covered with graffiti. She looked at all the markings and wondered vaguely if her name was scratched in nearby. Probably hers and Shelley's, Tara's, and Michelle's. The crew, the clique, the something like that. Then she wondered if Granddaddy ever found her name etched in the wood. Probably not 'cause she would have been busted if he had. Crystelle looked across the rows of long brown wood. They seemed to go on forever when Granddaddy first brought her here. She remembered that. She looked at the man and smiled. By his finger she could tell he was almost finished with the editorial page. She looked up and across again. Probably all her friends were etched in this wood. All the rumored loves, secret loves, and 2 true 2 be 4-gotten love. Maybe somebody had a fight. They could scratch in so and so's a whatever. Reading their words was a way to count time. 'LaToya and her whole crew is wack.' That was high school. 'Tyrone is a scrub.' That was middle school. 'Shannon's a jive turkey.' Elementary school. Everything that happened between her friends was carved in this wood. Some carved better than others. Or, did everyone just grow older and more skilled? When she looked down and felt the rough texture, the tables were full of schoolkids—boys looking for a girl to take home, girls looking for a boy to take to the prom. When Crystelle looked up again, only she and her grandfather were there.

"Granddaddy?"

"Hmmmm?"

"What time is it?"

"Just before half past, Crystelle."

"Ya'll got me up early. I slept hard all day yesterday."

"What time you get at work?"

"Ten or eleven."

"Day's almost over just a minute later."

"Not when you're working till just past ten that night."

"And goin' home to eat and sleep." He looked down at Crystelle. "You're not even washing your own dishes when you get home. And no kids too. Shoot." Granddaddy snapped his paper shut.

Just then a woman, must be older than Mamma because of the hair but not a wrinkle at all, appeared. "Can I do my job now, Paul?"

Crystelle rolled her eyes up to really see this woman who forgot to call her granddaddy Mr. Cole and why.

"You were doing your job when you gave it to me to read."

"I have to bind it." The woman shifted over to lean on her right foot, and her body rolled over with her.

"Don't like the binding."

The woman shifted to the left, rested her elbow on her left

hip, and held out her hand. "That's why I'm asking you if I can work, Paul."

"I'm sure you can, Lou."

Crystelle rolled over to her Granddaddy now, since in the corner of her eyes she could see his arm swinging from the back of the chair to where it just brushed the hem of ol' Lou's skirt. The woman's eyes were brown like the tables, her face brown like the scratches.

"This your granddaughter." Lou made a "you know men" face at Crystelle.

"Hi you doin'?" Crystelle nodded her head but didn't smile.

"Fine. I'm Miss Louise, honey. Your grandfather talks about you every time he comes by. How's that big job you got up there in New York? Paul says you be workin' real hard."

"Oh he does?"

"Sure, hey, I got a daughter 'bout to finally finish college soon. This year, I hope. You think I can give her your number? She don't know what she wants to do after she graduates."

"Neither do I."

"Huh?"

"I say, neither did I. Yeah, you can give her my number."

"All right then." Miss Louise lowered her chin and looked at Crystelle over the top of her spectacles. "I'll get it from Paul later," she said, as she slowly lifted her chin. "Let ya'll visit. Well, all right now. See you."

"See you."

Louise looked at Granddaddy. "Bye, Paul."

"See you, Lou Lou."

Crystelle watched Granddaddy watch her sway back to the information desk.

"Nobody comes in the library anymore?"

"Kids come after school. School started, you know." He was still watching Miss Lou Lou switch and sway.

"Seemed like it was always crowded to me."

Granddaddy turned around and faced Crystelle now. "You always came after school too. All these ladies practically babysat ya'll."

"I don't remember Miss Louise."

"She's new," Granddaddy smiled.

"She can't call you Mr. Paul or Mr. Cole? Mr. Something? Dag."

"Told her not to."

"Mm." Crystelle looked over the stacks. "Black History still over there?"

"Yup."

"What you been reading lately?"

"Celestine Prophesy, Embraced by the Light."

"Really, Granddaddy? What did you think of *Celestine Prophesy?*"

"Too Eurocentric. Kept looking for Peruvians on every page."

"Me too. Somebody who knew what was up."

"That's right, Crystelle Girl."

"Where's your posse?"

"Not too many of us left, Crystelle Clear." Granddaddy looked straight into her eyes, still smiling.

Crystelle looked away. "It's not the same here."

"No, but it ain't supposed to be."

Crystelle and her grandfather stood up. He winked at Ms. Lou Lou. Crystelle gave the space in front of her one last stroke, and fingertips felt the old brown wood. Crystelle let her hand fall. As she and Granddaddy walked toward the exit, she opened her fingers wide, feeling texture and time.

"This is nice, Crystelle." Granddaddy held his arm for Crystelle to link with her own as they walked and he talked. "You coming home for the holidays is too rushed."

"When's the last time we went to that old library together?"

"Years ago now."

"Mm."

"So much time stretched ahead for the rest of the day."

"Yeah."

"No presents to wrap, no cheap last-minute shopping to do."

"Yup," Crystelle laughed.

"Let's walk over to the park."

"Ya'll still playing chess over there?"

"Not too many of us left, Crystelle Clear," Granddaddy looked ahead, smiling.

Crystelle could see the age in his smooth brown skin. It was hanging a little loose, but it was hanging smooth. Granddaddy walked tall now. Taller than he had when he still smoked cigarettes. He walked with an old wooden cane, brown and carved like the old library tabletops. He walked slow, though. It was less than a stroll. With his loose shirt and loose shorts, anyone caring to notice would see his skinny legs, and the scar he got from a knife fight down South, and the places where muscles used to be. His silver crown, thick and wild, sat perfectly on his head. Dignified and still, his hair made him taller than Crystelle.

"What you looking at, girl?"

"You look good Granddaddy. Ol' Miss Louise probably thinks so."

"Ol' Miss Louise lookin' good too."

"How old is she?"

"Older than your Mamma. Old enough to be a grand-mamma, which she is."

"What?" Crystelle stretched the what out for as long as she felt amazement. "Yeah, Granddaddy, ya'll look good. Is that why you still been going to the library all these years—the lady librarians? I thought it was for the books."

"Shoot, did you go to college for just the books?"

Crystelle looked at the stone wall surrounding the park. Then she said, "Guys weren't really on my list," laughing. Then she looked back at Granddaddy.

"Well you were on theirs—at least one of 'em. So, you still seeing that boy Hemp."

"Hamp. Yeah."

They turned into the stone gate and sat near the dry fountain. Crystelle could hear a woman through the hedges reaching above her head. She could hear a cackle, a hock, a spit. Then, she could hear the woman talking to the pigeons, talking about a man that left her, right there behind the branches that were reaching, straining, over Crystelle's head. Granddaddy and Crystelle sat still for a minute.

Crystelle breathed a little more air.

"You walking too heavy, Crystelle."

The woman through the hedge stopped cackling to the pigeons. The dirty birds flew away, and she shifted her weight to stand. Crystelle could hear her mumble steadily disappear.

"Too heavy," Granddaddy repeated.

"What you mean heavy?" she whispered. She laughed with hands on hips, turned, facing him. She could still see the stone wall that wrapped around the park just past his head. It was covered, like the tabletops at the library, with tags. Paint sprayed by hands she knew. She looked at a pigeon sitting all alone, looking at Crystelle looking back at it. Then, she looked at her grandfather again. "You saying I'm fat?"

"No, not hardly. Fact is, you could stand to gain—put some meat on them bones of yours. I'm saying you're walking heavy."

Granddaddy was still looking straight ahead. She turned and leaned back. But she didn't say anything, so they just sat there for a while.

Crystelle knew it meant something powerful—she and her

granddaddy sitting without talking. She knew she could lean on his arm, if she wanted. Or, she could kiss his face. But, instead, she just sat. She could talk, but she didn't want to tell him about the third shadow. How could she describe last night and her face in the mirror and glass? The thoughts weren't straight.

She was thinking like a madwoman. Like the woman just behind the hedge, feeding pigeons and talking out loud to the sound of flight, to the birds she had just fed as they flew away. Crystelle wasn't like her. She was still going to work every day. But, she just hadn't gone yesterday, no, the day before yesterday. And the day before that. Yeah. All her feeling attached to thoughts like a weird cell formation—multiplying and multiplying inside of her, not quite formed into anything coherent. It was a mess, and it was chaotic. She could feel it growing inside her, and she had no idea what it might become.

Granddaddy let her know he could tell. So, Crystelle sat back in this place where he conjured ways to tell. And she listened. And she watched.

In the silence, she heard something. In the unchanging scene, she could see a little bit further. But, the sound was like a song whose words she forgot, whose singer she didn't know. And the things she saw became like a dream she struggled to remember but couldn't.

Crystelle cleared her throat. Then she sighed. "I could just lean up against you right now and sleep," she whispered.

"Naw, don't do that. You got too much work to get done."

"Hey, I'm on a little vacation down here, Granddaddy," Crystelle shoved against his arm, but the soft flesh didn't give.

"No you ain't. You wanna sit and talk, we can sit and talk. You wanna sit and just sit—that's fine too. But don't sit here lying to me, girl."

"Dag."

"Umph, that's what it is. You lying to me, you lying to you. You gotta get real to get right, Crystelle Clear."

Crystelle opened her mouth, but Granddaddy cut in before the words could come out.

"A dream can't do anything on it's own, Crystelle. It's what you do with a dream when you wake up that makes it power-ful."

"How you know I'm dreamin', Granddaddy?"

"I don't know." Granddaddy turned in his seat and looked at her, full on, for the first time that day. "Shoot. Don't know nothin'. But I do know this—you're either dreamin' or preg-nant or both."

"What you say?" Crystelle felt her question roar into the West Philly street, felt it echo down every street, felt herself scream.

Granddaddy squinted a little and cocked his head to one side, leaning in. "Quit whisperin', girl."

'Can't you hear me?' she heard her spirit call.

Crystelle opened her mouth wider, but instead of the sound of her own voice, she heard another cackle, another hock, and spit.

Granddaddy pulled back quick, and Crystelle caught a vision in the corner of her right eye. She blinked, closed her mouth tight. The homeless woman stood on the path in front of them. Wearing straight-leg, red, satin pants and matching red blouse, she looked like she hadn't changed clothes since the last dance at some 1982 disco. She had her hand on her hip and a cigarette slanted down the corner of her mouth. The woman opened two fingers like scissors ready to cut through the warm air between them. But they snatched the cigarette instead, and Crystelle realized the woman was wearing lip-stick. She tilted her fully-made face to the sun and blew a cloud of smoke into the sky, never once shifting her gaze away from Crystelle. The woman smiled, relaxed her fingers, held the cigarette a tease away from her smiling lips. With her other hand she scratched her hip, worked around her body, and down, scratching.

Granddaddy looked away, but Crystelle followed the scratching with her eyes. She could see the other hand, still poised with the burning cigarette. The hard digging now shifted under her red pants, slow and syncopated below her hips, under her red pants behind her. She pulled her hand out and snapped her fingers to the side, forming a sharp beat, even shook her hips to the new song, grinning, and put her hand back on her hip. Crystelle looked up into her eyes and the cheap powder above them, smudged and blue.

The woman winked, spit again, and walked away.

"Humph." Granddaddy shook his head. "Tell you this—they need to have a place for people like that. This park ain't no place for her."

Crystelle couldn't shift her stare away from the woman in red. Even as she walked away, Crystelle watched. She watched the woman along the winding path, the tap-slip tap-slip, tap-slip, of her unbuckled heels sounding long after Crystelle couldn't see her anymore. Crystelle looked down at the ground. Then up at the sky. Then back at the spot where the woman had stood and scratched and snapped. Crystelle's eyes, now a sullen glower, blinked.

By the time Crystelle could stop looking, Granddaddy had long stopped shaking his head. He was looking at his granddaughter, body shifted back against the park bench. Crystelle could see his eyebrows knitting together, closer and closer together, so she shook her head and laughed a little.

"Guess that woman put a kinda spell on me."

"Humph," Granddaddy said again, softer now, "don't tell no more tales, child."

Crystelle could see Granddaddy's eyes soften and shine in the afternoon sun.

"You believe in ghosts, Granddaddy?"

"Huh?"

Crystelle cleared her throat, tried to make an outside sound to match her spirit's screams just inside her face. "I say, do you believe in ghosts?"

"What you say? Ghosts?"

Crystelle nodded.

"What you asking me that for?"

"Why is everyone asking me why I'm asking?"

"Well, who else are you asking?"

"I asked Hamp."

"What did he say?"

"Nothing."

"Humph." Granddaddy shook his head, tapped his cane three times. "Has he been asking you what's wrong with you lately?"

"No, he hasn't been asking me anything like that. Why?"

"Has he been around? I mean, have you been seeing him lately?"

"Yeah, sure. All the time. Like, every day."

"And he hasn't been wondering why you take all this time off of work? Every time I call seems like you're sleeping . . ."

"What are you trying to say, Granddaddy?"

"Here and now I'll tell you, though I told you before too. You're walking too heavy, Crystelle Clear. Ever since you left college, since you graduated and moved up there to that city, New York, with that boy, Hamp."

"That city, that boy. That's my life, Granddaddy."

"Is it?"

Crystelle opened her mouth, but nothing came out.

"Is that your life? What is your life, Crystelle Clear? Tell me."

The sun kind of eased back into the Western sky. Crystelle could almost hear a sigh coming from the sun. "You believe in ghosts, Granddaddy?"

"Yeah, Crystelle." She looked up into his face as he spoke. "Yeah, girl. If you're talking about spirits, about ancestors and such, yeah. I believe." Crystelle smiled, and Granddaddy tapped his cane once. "But I also believe this," he continued. "I know the place where the past and the present come together and touch can be a dangerous one."

"Like a horror movie?"

"Naw, not like that at all. Like that lady over there. She so stuck in the past, there ain't no present. And this present is a gift, Crystelle Clear. Don't give up the gift of now."

Crystelle and Granddaddy just sat for a while. Sun seemed to hang in the same place, watching to see what would happen next.

"So what, you pregnant or what?"

"Why you keep asking me that, Granddaddy?"

"You sleep too much for a woman who ain't, that's why."

"Humph."

"Humph?"

"Just tired, that's all."

"Oh yeah?"

"Yeah, Granddaddy, just tired."

"From what? You get into work so late——"

"I stay late, too. That's how it is in New York. People don't work like they do in Philly."

"Oh, you're trying to tell me something about work? Well, I'll tell you something. Better yet, I'll ask you. When's the last time you did some?"

"Uh uh. You asked me that, Granddaddy?"

"Well?"

Crystelle tried to think back yet again in her mind. Just as she got past yesterday, she heard a new cackle from the homeless woman.

Granddaddy tried to pull himself up with his walking stick. Crystelle focused on the tussle going on a few yards away. To Crystelle's eye, two shadows struggled down the path leading toward her. One shadow stood over the other, chunky and square. The smaller figure struggled more, waved, gestured, prepared to strike.

"What the heck?" Granddaddy's voice trailed off as he stood up. Crystelle stood up too and bent her arm for Granddaddy to lean on. "Go on, girl," he said as he shifted over to his cane.

"You want me to go down there?" Crystelle leaned back as she spoke.

"Girl, go on down there. That ol' crazy woman is fixing to down my main man."

Crystelle squinted against the setting sun blazing through her eyes, frying the front of her brain. She raised a hand up to form a visor and took three steps forward.

"Go on, girl."

As Crystelle walked down the path away from Granddaddy, the two shadows slowly took on human form. The crazy disco lady balled both fists and danced like a cartoon character, pretending to box a man who was clearly struggling not to box back. Granddaddy was right—it was his good friend.

"Mr. Henry!" Crystelle called as soon as she saw him crack his fingers and bend his arm back.

"Girl, you comin' down here right on time," he called without ever taking his eyes off the crazy disco lady. "Someone better get this woman offa my back."

Crystelle ran forward now. "Okay," she said, as she put her hands on Mr. Henry's shoulders.

"I ain't the type to floor a woman," he declared, "but this sister is trying to vex me."

Maybe because she saw the look in Henry's eye, the crazy lady jumped back. "Ooooo, you!" she scolded, wagging her finger at the man three times her size.

"Lady," Henry dropped his arms and raised the tone of his voice, "I don't even know you."

"You tryin' to break them up," she slurred. "Let 'em be, let 'em be."

"What?"

"Let 'em be, let 'em sit and be."

"Awwwww!" Mr. Henry waved his hand down and toward the crazy lady in disgust and began to walk off, then turned one time like he had more to say. It seemed to Crystelle that all he could do was shake his head with one strong humph! and march away. Crystelle could see Granddaddy down the path, tipping as fast as he could toward her. Just as Crystelle turned, she flinched. The crazy lady touched her arm, softly. Crystelle could feel her nails lightly scratch her skin. It was an almost caress.

"He needs to leave ya'll alone, leave ya'll be."

"What you say?"

"He just gonna muckety muck the talk with nothin' worth saying."

This close Crystelle realized the woman was much older than she'd first imagined. One of those older Black women who you can tell must be older, but don't look it. She looked to be Mamma's and Aunt Brenda's age from a distance, but now she could easily be as old as Ms. Lou Lou, maybe even older. 'She must've been already old the first time she put on this outfit,' Crystelle thought. 'Must have put it on, decided she looked good—she still looked good—and simply never took it off.'

"You gotta get away from him."

"Huh?"

"Aw—he ain't bad, I ain't sayin' that. Just he gone muckety up the talk."

Crystelle peered into the woman's face. Her eyes glowed an almost green back at her.

"I know I wish my daddy or granddaddy or some hadda talked to me like that. Woulda been nice. Real helpful even. Ya'll gots to conversate—ya'll can conversate." The lady shook her head, took a side look at Crystelle, and mumbled, "Might be too late for ya anyhow. I hope not. I swear to the good God above I hope not, honey. But, could be too late. Ya neva know." The woman started to scratch, and Crystelle stepped back. The woman's rolling eyes snapped into Crystelle's, softened, then hardened.

"Humph," the woman sneered. "Whateva. I got my pigeons to talk to. I'm fine as wine. Ain't flinchin' for nobody—tell you that. Tell you that right now, girl. This here diva don't flinch. Not for no-bod-y."

Crystelle almost followed the woman as she walked off into the tangled, neglected bushes.

"Crystelle Clear!" she heard her Granddaddy call out.

Crystelle shuddered, turned, and walked back along the old park path to the bench. Granddaddy gave her a queer look as she approached the men. Crystelle smiled, Granddaddy sort of nodded back, and she stood over Granddaddy and Mr. Henry for a few minutes, listening to their talk.

After holding on so long, the sun finally dropped off of the edge of the sky. Like a kid who wanted to fight sleep to catch the grown talk in the next room, sun had been eavesdropping on the drama in the park. But, like all sleepy children, he couldn't fight his own natural rhythms, and dusk slowly took over, marking fresh time.

"Man, the moon must be coming in full tonight," Granddaddy laughed and tapped his cane three times.

"Aw, cuz, that chick," Mr. Henry's voice trailed off. "Like to vex me, cuz. Like to vex me somethin' bad."

"Hey, man, you got yourself open to that drama," Granddaddy laughed and tapped again, "walkin all through her park, like you thought it was yours."

"MmHm, she sho' was markin' her territory—like an ol' hound, an ol' she hound."

"Yeah, well," Granddaddy started to stand up, "let's step on outta here, before she starts howlin'."

"Well, I'm glad I got to see you, Crystelle, if only for a minute," Mr. Henry announced, as he stretched and stood up.

"Glad I could be of some service."

"Yeah, lil Crystelle, you came right on time, gal." Mr. Henry threw his arm around Crystelle's shoulders.

"You weren't gonna strike her though, were you?" Crystelle leaned her head back on Mr. Henry's arm as they walked ahead of Granddaddy.

"Dunno. Never been vexed like that before. Never hit a woman before, never even shook a woman up, not even a shove. But that chick. She liked to have me vexed." Mr. Henry's voice trailed off again. "Don't know Crystelle Clear. Don't know what I might've done."

As they walked slowly through the stone gate and out of the park, a flock of pigeons rose up, circled, then settled back down in the cluster of trees behind them.

Chapter Five

Hamp could feel the bass pump beats into his soul. He felt his body swagger, dip and slip and slide, as he walked through the lounge to the table where his boys were sitting. Women watched him. He smiled, not at them, but to himself. Back in the day he would have worked the male-female ratio to his favor, and the women definitely outnumbered the men this night. But he felt more than the beats in his soul. He felt Crystelle. Even with her sudden departure, even with the telephone conversation, even with the fact that they hadn't talked since the night before last, he still felt her. And when he could feel his love for her—even with all that—he knew he wouldn't need another woman ever again. He was done.

"What's up, man?" Hamp slapped the open palm extended toward him and clenched it into a tight fist. He pulled his boy up from the chair and, shoulders hunched, pounded Mike's back. The other men, mostly Kappas like himself, gave him pounds, nods, and what ups. Hamp's swagger never stopped, even when he stopped walking and sat still. His laid back self was still slick this night, and he felt more women glance his way.

"She has the goods tonight." Mike tilted his bottle toward the bar before he took a swallow and licked his lips. He kept two fingers around the neck of his bottle and rubbed the cool frost up and down the curve of glass with his thumb.

The men's heads swung in sync over to the long black bar. Hamp eyed the woman Mike was eyeing right away. Her red dress fit without looking tight over her hips. "Red isn't a color you see sisters wearing anymore," Hamp said.

"I don't know why," Mike leaned back. "She's got the goods for sure. All these other women are wearing black, but she wore red just to get my attention."

"You?"

"Yeah, man, I'm going to have to give her some Mighty Mike tonight." The men eased back and laughed, as Mike stood up and walked over to the bar.

Hamp watched the game play out for a while. Of course the sister tossed her head away from Mike as he approached—but she tossed it, letting her hair wave hello even when her back seemed to say good-bye. Mike eased up behind her, as close as he could without getting slapped, and let his body kinda breathe on hers for a moment. Then he leaned in to order a drink, and she had to twist to give him space. That's when he grinned, Hamp imagined with an offer to buy a round, and she slowly let her stool swivel his way.

Hamp chuckled and turned back to the table. He lifted Mike's bottle in a mock toast to his success and finished the strong ale Mike left behind. "How's it going, guys?"

"Work and women, man," Tom replied, his voice low and deep under the music and talk.

"That's what the city is—a strong cocktail," Hamp laughed.

The other men talked to each other, got up to mingle, would grab a girl to dance with words sweet and rhythmic like the sound all around them. Whenever they returned to recover, Hamp and Tom were still laid back and talking.

At one point Mike sauntered over and leaned in. "Yo, she has a friend."

"I'm cool," Hamp offered.

"Oh, is Crystelle popping her head out tonight?"

"No, she went home for the weekend."

"Aw, man, it's on then," Mike offered.

"Naw, I'm cool."

"Word?" Mike and Tom pulled back and raised their voices and eyebrows together.

Hamp shook his head. "Am I that scandalous?"

"Word." Mike patted him on the shoulder and headed back to the bar. Hamp and Tom watched him walk with the woman past the lounge area, over to the small dance floor. Even with the woman in red, they faded into the smoke and the cluster of dark bodies moving together.

"So, what's going on? Are you trying to be like me now?" Tom could lean back in his chair and still be heard. He was commanding in his seat, sure and solid.

"Aw, man, I've always wanted to be you when I grow up." The men laughed and clicked their glasses together. "Seriously, though," Hamp leaned in to talk. "You've got a nice thingy thing going on: wifey in Westchester, work on Wall Street—VP and all that, kids just a coming on strong." Hamp took a swig, looked at the moving mass beyond them both, and realized Mike had gotten lost out there with all those people. "Yes, it is definitely time to move on."

"Move it to the next level."

"Sure."

"I hear you, brother. I mean, when I pledged you up at State College we were both scandalous." The men laughed and toasted again. "There was much booty to be gotten. And I wanted my fair share."

"Me too. Then I met Crystelle. You met Lauren."

"And yet, there was still more booty to be gotten!"

The men laughed again.

"Yeah, man," Hamp shook his head, "I don't know how we got away with everything we were doing."

"Shoot, I didn't."

"Word?"

"Yeah, man. Lauren caught me out there a couple of times. Somehow reeled me back in each time and still managed to make me feel like I better never do any dirt ever again."

"But you did."

"I did. Got caught once more—enough to lose her for a while. A long while. I worked hard, Hamp. Getting her back was another full-time job for me. I had lots to prove. But, you know, I always knew I was the settling down type. I knew I had it in me."

"Yeah, but when did you know she was the one?"

"When I had some bank, man. Lauren is an expensive sister. I had to move her up here and move her in. She left her job in Philly to be with me—finally—so I had to take care of her for a while."

"Yeah, I'm ready to take care of Crystelle now—really take care of her."

"Man, she hasn't left you all these years."

"Exactly. Who else am I going to marry? She must be the one. And I'm feeling ready to plant my seed."

"Yeah, man, kids are great. But, they are work—another full-time gig."

"Crystelle will make such a good mother. She's really loving."

"I still can't believe she never caught you in your dirt, man."

"I'm a smooth cat." Hamp stood up. "Do you want anything from the bar?"

"Another brew. Thanks."

Hamp waited for a bartender to take his order. Tom was right—he was lucky Crystelle never caught him. But, he wasn't being real with Tom. He didn't slide by because he was slick. Truth be told, he wondered why Crystelle never noticed the late night calls to his dorm room. She would just sleep through them—through a whole conversation. She was always so laid back. So cool to his hot touch. He dug that. Other chicks threw themselves in his path. It was like Crystelle stepped out of his way, walked away from him. He had to go after her, just to make sure he wasn't missing something good. And then he got her. And he knew she wasn't playing hard to get with him. 'Cause the girls that play that game always lose. At some point, you got her, and that's it. She can't maintain anymore. But Crystelle, even when he got her, it felt like she was still hard to get. Something about a boy back in Philly—a boy that died, and yet he always felt like he was in competition with him. Mostly 'cause she never wanted to talk about it. Mystery, that's it. She was so mysterious. And blasé. He never stopped being intrigued. Never stopped trying to tap it right, get her to open her body, if she wouldn't open her mind. He knew he had her heart. She loved him. That much he knew. He knew, even though his mother didn't.

'Most women would be glad to have him,' she'd said. 'So why'd he want a woman who acted like she didn't?' Talked about him to his sister, as if he wasn't even there. 'So, when's the wedding?' Mamma had finally thrown his way.

He hadn't asked Crystelle yet. Not for real. Every time he would bring up marriage she would slap the conversation away. A light slap to back him up. Without even lifting her eyes, much less her hand. But he felt it. Felt it up at Martha's Vineyard on that tiny, rocky beach. There was the ring, a real rock, right there in his bag. But she was so far off, even though they were right next to each other. He touched her, knew she liked it, but felt like she might not miss it if it were gone.

The bartender finally popped two caps, and Hamp walked back to the table.

"Funny how we both met our wives in college."

"Slow down, Hamp, you aren't even engaged yet. Have you asked her?"

"Almost."

"Well, you aren't married until you say I do. Trust me. It takes effort to walk down the aisle."

"She walks down the aisle, man."

"But you both have to walk back up."

"I hear that. But it is funny—out of the chapter, you and I are with our college girls."

"Man, Lauren wasn't letting me graduate and move on without her. She got her BS and then got her MRS, before she finished her MBA."

"Yeah. But we got them too."

"Yes. That's true. Other brothers were trying to step to my girl."

"No, not that. I mean, I felt, at least, like I got Crystelle. I had to chase her down."

"Well, your girl's a distant kind of person. She'll hang out with the girls, but she maintains her space. She never pledged, and I know for a fact Lauren wanted her to try to get on line with her."

"Yes, but I never would've crossed without her."

"And that's definitely worth rewarding, man." Tom dropped his bottle back and let the almost warm beer roll down his throat. For the first time he looked down while he was talking. "She doesn't socialize much." Tom's words came out like he was sitting in his office, like the dull glow of fluorescence steady beating above his desk.

"So she's always there for me when I get home."

Hamp had heard what he said, but he'd missed the way he

said it. Tom let his head fall down more, released full from his shoulders. Then he looked back up again. "So, sounds like your personalities work together." It was more a question than a statement, and Hamp didn't answer. The moment of silence following it lasted too long.

Tom forced a laugh and let the rhythm of his words shift back to match the blinking lounge lights. "Like how I knew Lauren wanted me—had claimed me—even when she acted like she didn't. I needed that to keep me going after her back then."

"Yeah, I guess that's it. I feel like I still have to get her. I'm still chasing her down."

"What's that Isley's song?"

"What one?"

"Insatiable Woman. That's what you have."

"Yes—she keeps me working." Hamp gulped down a dose of beer. "That's what it is."

He didn't finish that bottle. Hamp shifted in his seat a few times, then stood up. He needed to call his woman. He reached out to give Tom another pound and turned, but Tom didn't let him go.

"Hey, man, it's early. The night barely started. Where're you going?"

"Gotta go—"

Hamp turned around, but Tom held his grip, forcing Hamp to look at him one more time. "Yo," Tom said, steady and sure, "whenever you need to build, you know you can call me."

"Word, man." Hamp smiled, even though Tom's face was set on serious. "Thanks."

Hamp didn't say anything else, so Tom let him go. And then he was out.

The evening colored him in cool indigo—his suit and skin matching tall steel reaching to nearly night above—as Hamp stepped out of the club. When he managed to hail a cab, he flipped on his cell phone and checked his messages—nothing from her at home or on the voice mail at work. He dialed the 215 number he'd memorized in college. Just as he was about to hang up, Crystelle's mother's voice clicked on the machine. Hamp hung up without leaving a message. Even if Crystelle's mother had answered the phone, he wouldn't have asked her where Crystelle was. Years ago he'd learned he would never get that answer from her. Only an "I'm not sure," Space between each word. I'm. Not. Sure. Like a question thrown back for him to answer because her question wasn't where her daughter was, but whether he would keep trying to find her. Long, drawn out, and up on the sure. Like a song. Crystelle's Mamma could be mysterious too.

Hamp turned the key in his own apartment, flipped on the living room light, and sunk into his white, leather couch. The ring box sat right there on the coffee table in front of him. If only she'd come up to his place for once. Maybe surprise him by coming uptown; she'd see then what he'd been trying to ask for so long. He stood up and paced back and forth along the parquet floors. He lay down on the couch and flipped on the TV, intending to call back in a few hours, before 10:30.

He was surprised that he had fallen asleep when his telephone rang. He picked it up like a schoolboy in love, like he was a kid again, before the days of call waiting and voice mails, before the jangle of beepers and pagers and email alerts. Like it was the days, back in the days, when all you had was three television channels, one phone line, and a silence that said you were waiting for love to call.

Instead of Crystelle's voice, he heard Mike's slur. "Yo, man, we're coming up."

Even the giggle behind him was thick and sloppy.

"Wha?"

"Buzz me, man, we're in your lobby now."

"Naw, man, I'm chilling tonight—"

"Hey, Hamp, these sisters are from Penn State too—just a few years behind us. They remember you and want to say hey."

"Who?" Hamp heard the loud creak as the door to his building opened.

"Aw, thanks—" Hamp heard Mike talking away from the phone and a shuffling sound as one of his neighbors stepped out and let Mike in. Then Mike's voice turned echo-ey, and Hamp knew he was in his lobby. "Yo, we're in—on our way." Then he hung up.

Hamp paced three more times before he took the ring box back to his room and threw it in his dresser drawer. Then he heard his doorbell.

* * * *

Crystelle slipped out from under Mr. Henry's heavy arm. The weight of his muscles made her neck ache. A heavy, dull thud of pain shot up along the sinews connecting her skull to her spine.

"Want a hoagie, baby girl?" Mr. Henry asked.

"No, I need to see some friends. You know I'm making dinner, right Grandaddy?"

"Okay, Crystelle Clear. I won't eat too much. Shoot, won't eat nothin'. Ain't got no money to be givin' to these people." Granddaddy kissed her on her cheek and followed Mr. Henry into the take-out joint.

Crystelle rolled her head back and forth and around, trying to crack it. She followed the sidewalk, rubbing with her thumbs under her ears, walking alone through the rose-colored dusk. She passed a couple of boys who looked at her, smirked to each other, then laughed when she plodded away.

Crystelle tried to see what they saw: She was walking with her fingers splayed up against her head, her thumbs anchored under her skull. And she was walking slowly. With both arms bent up and out, her elbows pointed on two different directions in the world. But the rubbing took away the ache, made her feel better. She didn't care what she looked like. As the pain disappeared she could let her arms hang to her sides, anyway. And she walked faster, at a normal pace. Their laughter disappeared as she turned a corner.

She turned and walked into Jimmie's smiling face. He looked back like he was waiting for her to tease him, to say something. Almost real. She breathed out into the empty air surrounding her heart and whispered into the folds of warm night draping her round shoulders, 'Rest in peace, J.' She glanced away from the face on the wall, away from the empty lot turned community garden. The boys (how many of them were now men?) had spray painted RIPJ under his smiling face. That face would never change. It was caught, grinning, against the red brick. Forever. Well, maybe one day the mural would fade, Crystelle thought, as she turned another corner and walked down Frazier Street, feeling the aloneness of the night until she heard the simple, sweet sound of friendship.

"Hey, you!" Shelley stood on her stoop, smiling, then waving and smiling, then down her stoop bouncing. Bouncing and smiling, the baby was waving too.

Crystelle looked up and heard the bone at the base of her neck crack at the sudden shift. Her baby is so big, she thought, as all three smiled and bounced together, toward each other, on Frazier Street.

"I heard you came home!" Shelley called out, her voice like the sample of an old school song. Established rhythms under new words.

"Who's telling my business?" Crystelle laughed back.

"Your Mamma!" Shelley sent out.

"MmHm. Must have told Mouth Almighty." Crystelle and Shelley stood facing now. They could have touched, but they didn't.

"Ms. Shirley," they whispered together, and the baby laughed again and hugged with them. They hugged long and tight now.

"Uh huhhh! How old is he?"

"Girl, 19 ½ months."

"Wow."

"Yeah."

"Lemme." Crystelle held out her arms.

"Go to your Auntie."

Crystelle could feel the baby rest comfortable against her soft chest. "Hey, Jibri," she cooed. As she nuzzled his soft brown skin, she smelled his fresh little boy smell. "He's still wearing diapers?"

"Oh, yeah," Shelley looked surprised.

"I don't know nothin' 'bout raisin' no babies!" Crystelle did her best Butterfly McQueen.

"Guess not," Shelley laughed. "No, they stay in diapers for a minute or two longer. He's always trying to take it off, though. I talk to him about how uncomfortable it feels, and I tell him he has a potty, if he wants to go like the big people."

"Does he use it?"

"Pretends to so far."

"Wow."

"Yeah. It's a lot, and you have to be real patient."

"Wow. How does it feel, Shelley?"

"Like it's a lot and you have to be real patient." She smiled.

"MmMm!" Crystelle hit Shelley's arm.

"No, I'm kidding." Jibri grasped Shelley's finger as he rested on Crystelle's hip. Shelley pushed out her lips for a moment, then looked at Crystelle with eyes soft and easy. "You know, I'm not kidding. It is a lot, girl. And you do have to be real patient. But, when the day is done and I see him sleeping, or when he decides he wants a hug, or just, whenever, you know—little moments. It's so worth it, Crystelle. Really, it is wonderful."

Crystelle kissed Jibri on the cheek. "He's so big."

"Like his daddy."

"He comes around a lot?"

"Every day."

Crystelle could see Mel, towering, with wide hands and thick flesh. They were hands meant to hold a baby. Cushy and strong and steady too. They were hands that would make a baby feel safe. "That's good. He's a good man."

"I'm thankful."

"Ya'll gonna get married?"

"Probably. Long as he doesn't make any more out here."

"I hear you. Hey, I have to make dinner. Mamma's going to be home soon. Why don't you come over while I cook? We can talk."

"Sounds good. Wait a minute." Shelley ran in and called to her mother.

"Crystelle's home?" She heard from the back of the house, so she climbed the stoop with Jibri still in her arms. Shelley took him so Crystelle could hug the boy's grandmother.

"Girl, you look kinda tired."

"Traveling, working—you look good though."

"Well I thank you. New York treating you rough?"

"I'm trying to make it happen."

"I hear that. You got a man up there?"

"Yeah."

"He good to you?"

"Yeah."

"Good. I don't want to have to drive all the way up there just to hurt somebody." Crystelle laughed with Shelley's mom. "All right now. I'll see you later."

"See you."

"Tell your mom I said hey," she said, as she turned and walked back in the house.

"Okay."

Shelley carried Jibri as they walked a few houses from home to home. Jibri reached out and touched Crystelle's hair, decided to yank it, then pulled his hand back.

"Oh, that reminds me," Crystelle said as she turned her key, "I was wondering—"

"—if I could do a 'do?"

"Girl, I can't take this stuff much longer."

"You look like you wanna go natural."

"I don't want to cut it. Girl, I can't do that," Crystelle laughed, as she pushed her front door in. "I want to get braided."

"Cornrows with beads and tin foil on the edges?" Shelley grinned.

"No, girl, no beads."

"So you want braids. Your hair is real long still."

"Yeah, but feel."

"Kinda stiff."

"It needs a break."

"Or, do you want a break from doing it?"

"My hair and I need a break from each other. I ain't doin' it no good."

"Mm, well, that's a session."

"Please, Shelley, please." The streetlight on the corner flickered, almost went out, then glowed up to bright. "Please, Shelley, please, Shelley, please Shelley, Shelley, Shelley, please."

"Uh uh," Shelley shook her head and giggled. "I'll do it. I just don't know when."

"Let's do it tonight."

"You have to wash and dry it first."

"Once the food is going, I'll jump in the shower real quick."

The two women stood at Crystelle's threshold. Jibri squirmed in Shelley's arms. Crystelle kissed him in the space between his eyes.

"Well, look, let me go on home, eat, and put Jibri to bed. I'll swing by later."

"All right, girl."

"Peace," Jibri said, as Shelley turned and held his hand to wave good-bye.

Crystelle boiled rice, threw a pan of seasoned chicken into the oven, and made enough salad for four. She checked the machine in Mamma's room—no blinking light—as she struggled out of her clothes and jumped into the shower.

Mamma, Granddaddy, and Crystelle were still eating in Granddaddy's front room when Shelley walked up the stoop and came right in.

"There's food left in the kitchen, honey," Mamma said between bites.

"Oh, I just ate."

"Where's my main man?" Granddaddy asked. "Girl, don't be comin' round here without my main man."

"He's home asleep."

"He can sleep here. Shoot, babies can sleep anywhere. Go get him."

"Daddy, Shelley is not gonna walk all the way back home, wake that baby boy up, drag him out in this night air, and bring him all the way back down here just so you can make him cry."

"And then ignore him the rest of the night," Crystelle cut in.

"Awwww!" Granddaddy waved his hand in the air, then laughed at the TV. Mamma rolled her eyes and winked at Shelley.

As soon as Crystelle loaded the dishwasher after dinner, she plopped down between Shelley's knees. Eventually Mamma, then, even later, Granddaddy went upstairs to bed. Shelley had finished half of Crystelle's hair by then. Crystelle would hand up a clip, hold a section of hair with her hand, take the comb and hold it in the air by her ear. Shelley would part and twist, gathering Crystelle's hair like silk. The rhythm was silent and regular, and the night took on a new softness. Shelley hummed a little, and soon the humming turned to words that the two women shared in the easy space between them.

Crystelle was breathing out thoughts she hadn't shared with anyone. Simple thoughts that no one heard because no one was around when she'd been thinking them. "He thinks I don't know. But I know. I know what he wants next."

"Crystelle, ain't nothin' wrong with a man wanting to marry you."

"I know." Crystelle tried to lift her head a little, but Shelley nudged it back down. "He just isn't filling me up."

"Filling you up? With what?"

"With—I don't know."

"Girl, he's got money. He looks good. He loves you. He loved you before you even loved him. I remember seeing ya'll together up at State College. He was all over trying to get with you—all over it. You say he still calls, comes over, wants to be with you. I don't see a problem."

Crystelle turned her head to the side, so Shelley could move down the full length of her hair. They were quiet for a minute.

"How did you find out you were pregnant, Shelley?"

"Missed a period."

"You always keep track?"

"I do when I'm with a man."

"Like you've had so many." Crystelle cut her eyes to look up into Shelley's face just as Shelley turned to grab the brush behind her. She pulled it against Crystelle's ends without saying anything. After those strands were brushed and braided, Crystelle spoke up again. "Well, I don't keep track."

"Girl, that would drive me crazy. I know it drives your gynecologist crazy. What do you do when they want to know when your last period was?"

"I just make up a date for her."

"I do that when I'm single, but not when I'm getting some on the regular. I need to know what's goin' on with my body."

Crystelle could feel Shelley moving up the last few loose sections of her head. Soon she would gather all her hair, twisted up to her crown, and pin it together. Shelley called this style a basket of love. It was a name she'd gotten from a picture book she bought for Jibri before he was even born.

"So, what was it like?"

"What?"

"When you found out."

"You mean when he found out. He told me, really. I was thinking, "Dag, am I late?" And he just stopped by like 'yo, where's your period?' "

"What?"

"Yeah, girl."

"So what did you say?"

"I said, 'Baby, I don't know where it is.' "

"Uh uh—were you scared?"

"Not really, I always knew he loved me. But let me finish."

"There's more?"

"Yeah, so get this. Guess what that brother had with him that day."

"What?"

"A kit."

"What?"

"Can you believe it? He was like 'go on and take care of business. I'll be right back.' And I was like 'yo, where are you going?' And he said, 'I'm hungry. I'm getting some food.' And he jetted."

"So what did you do?"

"Went to the bathroom. So, I'm thinking he's going to get a cheese steak or probably something from the corner store, right."

"Right."

"He comes back—before the test was even ready—he comes back with a bag of food."

"Wait, how long did the test take?"

"Well, I didn't take it right away. I was mad he left. Then I felt like, how'd he know to bring me a kit? I gave myself a minute or two to remember he's a good man, I guess. Or, I was just scared, girl. I was studying for midterms. I don't know. Anyway, all I know is, he came back with a bag of groceries. He looked at me. I told him we needed a few more minutes, and he just started putting all the food in the ice box. He made food for both of us."

"What about the test?"

"Girl, I was upstairs watching the stick, while he was making whatever it was he was making."

"Clearblue Easy."

"Yes it was."

"So, what then?"

"He came up, saw the stick, and told me to come on and eat something."

"That's it?"

"That's it. He asked me what I was going to do about

school. I said I guessed I would have to stop for a while. He said his mother could watch the baby sometimes so I could still take classes."

"His mother doesn't work?"

"Nope."

"Why don't you just live there?"

"'Cause I have a mamma. Plus, it's too hectic over there. His cousins all over the place."

"Does she watch Jibri for you?"

"This semester I'm only taking two classes, but, yeah, she takes him all day Tuesday and Thursday for me."

"That saves money."

"Yeah."

Waves of muted light rolled off the television—a fluttering circle that just caught the two women in silhouette for a lone woman walking the street outside. She saw them, touching and whispering and leaning and wrapped in what looked like a love embrace, as she scratched under her arm and tap-slipped away.

"Are you on welfare?"

"Yeah, those checks last less than a minute, but I wouldn't be able to finish school without them, so I'm thankful."

"When are you gonna get that Temple degree, girl?"

"Probably in May. I'm going full time in spring, since Jibri can go to Head Start."

"Won't you have to go to school with him some days?"

"Yeah, with Head Start you have to, but I would want to anyway. Mel said he could work his hours and still go once a week too."

"Big Mel."

"Big Mel comes through for his little boy."

"Does he come through for his little boy's mamma?"

"I told you, girl. Every day."

"So you're straight."

"I'm straight. We're making it."

"When are ya'll gonna get married?"

"Probably when I finish school and get a job teaching. We can't afford to just yet."

"Do you talk about it?"

"Don't have to. He brought the kit over—remember?" Shelley rubbed her hands up Crystelle's head and held one hand over the bun she'd formed. "Some things you just know." She sat back on the old couch.

Crystelle felt the full sweep of neat rows Shelley had fashioned out of the wild mix of chemicals and new growth. Then she stood up to look in the mirror. "Oh, this looks good, Shelley. How long do you think it'll last?"

"As long as you take care of it, it'll last a long time."

"All right."

Crystelle plopped down on the other end of the couch. She flipped the stations on the television a few times. "I knew you were gonna come down this weekend," she heard Shelley mumble. "Even before your Mamma told me, I knew you would come." Then she heard Shelley snoring softly. Crystelle pulled a blanket out of the closet and over both of them. She flipped stations a few more times, felt Shelley turn over once. She knew she could wake her friend up and talk more. She wanted to talk about Hamp, about her own belly. Then she decided she could let her friend sleep, talk to Hamp. She could tell him everything, about the firm feeling growing inside her. About not knowing for sure. Maybe even about her dreams. Why not curl up and talk to him all night long? She eased off of the couch, away from the waves of light and into the darkness that had taken over the house. She felt her way to the back and picked up the kitchen phone. Now the only light on Crystelle's face were the numbers that turned dark again as she pressed them in.

* * * *

When Hamp heard his bell, he thought about not answering. He paced a few more times as Mike jangled it over and over, then pounded. "Come on, man!"

From the dark quiet of his own apartment, Hamp could hear his neighbor open a door, then close it quickly. The women's giggles were turning into laughter, getting louder and louder.

He turned on the light switch. "I knew I should have moved into that doorman building," Hamp said, as he unlocked his door and pulled Mike in. "Yo, man, are you bugging?"

"I tried to tell him to shhhh," the woman in the red dress said. "I tried to tell them both." She extended her hand as she spoke. "Hi, I'm Dora."

Hamp's hand automatically shook hers, but he was still focused on Mike, who fell in the couch and belched.

"Yo," Hamp paced two times, "you have to be out. I am not trying to hang tonight, man."

"What's wrong?" Dora tried to put her hand on Hamp's shoulder, but he paced away from her.

"I'm not having this tonight, man," he continued, ignoring her. "I have things I need to take care of."

"All right man, all right," Mike tried to stand up, then laughed. Dora looked at Hamp, saw he wasn't laughing, and decided not to laugh either.

"Come on, ya'll," she said, still looking at Hamp, "let's go." The women started to gather themselves and head toward the door.

Mike rolled his head along the back of the couch. "All right," he said in the moment of silence that was pulsing through the whole apartment. "Just give me a minute." He struggled up and stumbled down the hallway. The two women looked at each other and giggled again, as he fell into a framed print on Hamp's wall and rushed into the bathroom.

Hamp and the two women stood silently for a moment, watching the picture—a man and a woman in an outline of Africa—swing back and forth until it finally rested, crooked, against the wall. "You two might as well have a seat," he offered. "He might be a while." As the women sat down, he offered his hand. "I haven't even gotten your name yet."

"Hi, Hamp, I'm Wanda," she smiled up at him.

"You two do look familiar. Mike said you went to Penn State."

"Yeah," Dora leaned back against Hamp's cushions as she spoke. They were pillows Crystelle had gotten for him when he first moved in. "We were sophomores when you were graduating, so you might not remember us."

"But we remember you—all you guys," Wanda cut in.

"Ah." Hamp didn't quite know what to do with the tone in Wanda's voice. Should he know them? Had he known them? Had they been laid back, just like this, years ago, after a party, waiting for him and his boys? Back in his wild for the night days? He shook his head and walked into the kitchen. He needed to call his woman.

"Do you want something to drink?"

Wanda and Dora glanced at each other. "Um, I better check on Mike," Dora offered.

Wanda stood up and walked toward the kitchen. She rested her hand on one of two leather chairs in the space where a dining room table should have been.

"Mike," Dora tapped on the bathroom door. "You okay in there?"

Mike didn't answer. Wanda took a step toward her friend, then looked back through the kitchen doorway at Hamp, who was leaning against the spotless stovetop, staring at the wall in front of him.

Wanda shrugged at Dora. "Maybe we should just go," she mouthed. She knew they should have stayed at the lounge. She'd done everything she could to get Hamp's attention there. She wasn't trying to chase some other woman's man down for the night. She'd heard he and Crystelle were still together. Now she knew. She wasn't in college anymore. She didn't have time to waste just messing around. The only time she had over here was the time to go.

Hamp brushed past her on his way back to the bathroom. "Come on, man." He knocked on the door. "It's going on 11:00." Pretty soon it would be too late for him to call Crystelle.

"Aw, man." Mike heaved again, then spit. "Don't be a punk."

"Let me try," Dora put her hand on Hamp's waist and slid up next to him, with her back against the door. Hamp felt the light brush of her hips and jerked back from her. In the space his body created, Dora turned to the right and caught Wanda glaring. Dora turned to face the door now, so Wanda wouldn't see her smile, and leaned in, making Hamp back up even more.

Everyone heard a groan from the bathroom. Dora giggled. She glanced at Wanda and winked.

"Mike," Dora called softly. "Are you ok? Wanda and I need to go on now. Are you coming with?" Dora bent down to talk near the doorknob. This time Hamp didn't back up. Their bodies weren't touching, but with one shift in her hip, Dora would be up against him.

Wanda took another step toward the bathroom, then hung back. He wasn't even available for them to scramble over, she reminded herself.

"Excuse me," Hamp raised his arm, and Dora stepped to the side. "Yo, man," he knocked. "Let's go. I have to make this call now."

"Aw, man," Hamp heard Mike vomit into the toilet. "Ugh."

Hamp leaned back against the hallway wall in frustration. A minute passed before anyone said anything.

Hamp stepped to the door to open it, and Dora felt his body ready to shift, even before he moved forward. She quick-stepped and leaned in front of him. As he gripped and turned the doorknob, her hips bounced against the door. Her own weight pushed her in and over Mike's legs. Hamp twisted forward to try to catch her but missed as he caught himself against the force of her fall. Dora twisted forward and felt Mike heave under her, her own body moved against his chest, and she tried to stand as Mike jumped and turned. With one hand on the side of the tub and the other on the toilet rim, Mike pushed himself up. Dora only wiggled. Her heels slipped on the green tile, and she collapsed back on top of Mike; her cheek mashed against the white porcelain, even though he tried to catch her as she fell once again.

Mike felt his stomach churn and a fresh burn drive up his insides to his throat. Dora slapped the damp forehead against her other cheek, as he tried to struggle above her and lean into the toilet bowl. Bells echoed over the sound of Mike's body convulsing and heaving and Dora's sudden scream.

At Dora's shriek Wanda danced down the hall. She leaned over Hamp, eyes wide. In the space of time before the next ring, everyone froze in a trapped silence.

Dora looked up at her, and Wanda watched a glob of Mike's puke drip from Dora's hair into her open mouth. Wanda felt her own bubbles popping into giggles—hot and funky from the champagne Mike had plowed them with earlier. She half-hoped Dora would throw up too, as she stood shaking and burping over Dora's ruined dress and hair.

Vomit slid down Dora's nose as she slapped and pushed Mike off of her. Each shove sent a gathering wave of nausea steaming out of Mike's raw throat.

Wanda was laughing so loud that she didn't hear the phone ring the second time. Then she saw Hamp pacing again. He headed to the bedroom, then came back and told everyone to hush. Wanda put her hand over her mouth. But Mike wasn't finished. He was shifting under and over Dora at the same time, tangled, trying to get to the bowl in front of him. Dora's screams kept coming. The more she struggled to get away from Mike, the more she pinned herself under his bulky frame. Wanda gave up. There was no way she was going to stop laughing now.

Hamp tried shutting his bedroom door on ring three, but the screams and laughter followed him inside. He looked at his clock shift closer to 11:00. If he didn't pick up now, his voice mail would click in, and he'd have to wait until tomorrow to call her back. As the fourth ring started to chime, Hamp clicked on the cordless.

"Hey, Crystelle?"

"Hi, baby. How'd you know it was me?"

"Baby, I'm so glad you called. I lo—"

Just then Wanda burst into his bedroom, laughing and carrying Dora's cries in with her. "Hamp, I am so sorry, but you need to come out here right now."

Hamp palmed the mouthpiece with all his strength. "What?" But he knew what was going on without asking. Dora was cussing like a sister from the streets, but Mike's groans were practically drowning her out. Hamp could just imagine the amount of vomit they were getting all over the place.

"You better come quick," Wanda managed between her own bursts of glee. "She looks like she's ready to go to blows."

"Damn!"

Hamp heard Crystelle on the other end. "Hello! Hello." Her tone was going down. Any minute now she would just hang up.

"Baby," he pleaded. "I'm—"

"You're—?" Crystelle sounded like his own mother. Just in that minute, he felt like a small boy in trouble again.

"Baby, I—"

"Hamp, come on," Wanda was still laughing, but her voice shifted into something seductive. "Come out here now," she called and slipped out of his room, leaving the door wide open.

Hamp slammed it after her. "Crystelle, baby—"

"Uh uh. What? Who is over there?"

"It's some friends of Mike's, honey—"

"Some friends of Mike's? Why are they at your apartment, if they're friends of Mike's?"

"Baby, he brought them by—"

"Who?"

"What?"

"You heard me. Who? Who is over there?"

"I don't even know these chicks, baby. Really. Mike brought them by—"

"What makes him think he can bring women over there, Hamp? Tell me that. How'd they get into your apartment? They didn't magically morph into your apartment did they? Who let them in?"

"Baby, lemme—"

"Uh uh. Baby? Uh uh."

Crystelle—"

"Uh uh, who is it?"

"What?"

"Who are they? Who is that over there?"

"Some chicks Mike knows."

"Mike knows from where?"

"I don't even know, baby. Mike says they went to Penn State—"

"Who? Who, Hamp? Give me their names."

"Ah, I think one said her name was Wanda, and the other is named, I think she said Dora."

"Uh uh."

"Baby, I——hello?" Hamp clicked off the phone. "Damn!" He didn't even hear her hang up. She just clicked off, ever so lightly, like they had kissed good-bye. "Damn."

Hamp didn't sleep again that night. He got rid of Dora and Wanda right away. Then he watched Mike half clean his own vomit. After he got Mike downstairs, hailed a taxi, and told the driver where to take him, Hamp went back upstairs and washed down his bathroom. He packed a few shirts and socks in a duffel bag, called his garage around the corner, and told the attendant to bring his car up for him. Finally Hamp glanced around, hearing, for the first time, his own deep breath. He tipped the picture frame, setting it straight again. Then he headed out.

The elevator doors opened as soon as Hamp pushed the arrow pointing down, and he stepped in. One foot rested on the carpet in the hallway; the other on the carpet in the tiny cube that was blinking lights and sounding chimes to lure him in and whisk him down. Both Hamp's feet were facing forward; his face was looking back. Metal doors separating the two spaces closed in, bounced against his twisted shoulders, and closed in again. He dropped his duffel bag between the beeping doors, ran back into the apartment, fumbled through the dark, and grabbed the ring box in his dresser drawer. As he rushed back out, he brushed against the print he'd just tipped into place. When his key turned the locks and the elevator fell away, the image swung, back and forth, back and forth, back and forth, three times, before it stopped, crooked again, against the white wall. Then silence entered his home, lingered, stayed.

I met my boyfriend at the candy store

He bought me candy, he bought me cake

He brought me home with a bellyache

Mamma, Mamma, I feel so sick

She called the doctor

quick, quick, quick

Doctor, Doctor, will I die?

Count to five and you'll be just fine

1, 2, 3, 4 . . .

—African American hand-clapping song

Chapter Six

Gray steel slid behind her and locked into place. Bolts rolled along caverns hewed deep in solid bulk, and her spirit leaped away. Aunt Brenda reached to link her arm with Crystelle's, and together the two women walked into the waiting room at Eastern State Pen. Quiet rushed through the stale air that hung like four walls around them. Crystelle's pupils swelled, the distension almost bulging, as Aunt Brenda pulled an envelope out of her black purse. Blue ink along white paper blurred, almost disappeared.

"I got this letter last week." Brenda's fingers reached into the split paper, pulled out more white, more blue. Lines and lines of blue against white. All the way down. "Think he woulda sent it sooner. I know they got calendars up in here."

Crystelle felt her spirit tip up behind her, lean over the plastic orange chair, whisper in her ear. "Why we here, Aunt Brenda?" it said. She said.

"I need to talk to this boy again." Brenda handed the letter to Crystelle.

Crystelle felt one of the white sheets cut into her finger. She looked at the tiny flap of skin hanging over the place where flesh had been torn away. Then she pressed her torn finger against her lips, licked the slit with her tongue, sucked blood.

Crystelle sat there, with her finger in her mouth, until she almost dropped the letter in her other hand. She looked down at the words, blinked, felt her spirit twist and fly.

Dear Mrs. Johnson,

I feel kinda funny calling you that since I known you all my life. You used to call me off the block when it got late or we got too loud. You used to feed me at the block parties we used to have back on Frazier Street. I miss those times, but prison will teach you one thing and that is that you can't go backwards in time. But I do want to go back. I want to go back

The page blurred again and Crystelle looked up, saw Manny and them. Manny on the block. Manny in the park. Manny bum-rushing to get on the bus. Manny standing over her, eyes blinking once, twice, three times, before he dropped down, stood up, backed away, ran. Manny running that night, running as her spirit broke out to chase him down. To stay with Jimmie. To chase him down. Onto Market Street. Under the el. Chase him down. Stay. All her life, too.

Crystelle's head rolled back, then snapped up, as Aunt Brenda pulled the sheets of white away.

"Don't need to read it, if you don't want to. It says he wants out, basically." Brenda folded the pages back into the envelope, put the envelope back into her purse. "Says he wants out."

The two sat still, watching families come in. Young women with kids, older mothers, men who kept their heads down and their eyes off to the side.

"I saw his mamma the other day. Saw her at the new Rite Aid they built. We just saw each other, though I suspect she'll be calling me later tonight or comin' around the house or something."

Aunt Brenda sighed, put her arm around Crystelle's shoulders. "I feel for her. I do. Manny wasn't all bad. He was a good kid most of the time. She did her best with those boys."

A woman in uniform motioned to Brenda. She stood up. "You comin'?"

Crystelle reached out, took the black purse in her Aunt Brenda's hand, and looked up into her face. She couldn't rise.

"I'ma be right back then."

Crystelle watched Brenda's hips and back stiffen as she walked away. The roll of flesh she was used to seeing switch locked up against Benda's spine. She walked like a woman with no flesh, a woman in stone.

When her Aunt Brenda disappeared through a buzzing door, Crystelle gazed around at faces blank like hers. At little kids running around until their mothers slapped them on their behinds. At men slouched and older women who looked like mammas sitting up straight. Just like Aunt Brenda. She sat for what felt like a long time, but it was less than an hour.

Crystelle looked up at Brenda again, looked as she took the black purse back. "How was it?" Crystelle whispered, but Brenda was already pulling out her keys and turning to go, walking away when Crystelle was just standing up.

'She ain't said boo.' Crystelle leaned back to hear her spirit tip closer. 'She must be mad. She didn't have boo-sqwat to say. Dag.' Crystelle nodded, felt her spirit's hand in her own and followed Aunt Brenda out.

When she walked through the double doors, Brenda was gathering both their ID's and signing out. Crystelle followed her through the green halls to the parking lot. When they stepped outside, Brenda pulled on her sunglasses and jangled her keys, her hips slowly unlocking, almost rolling by the time they reached her car.

"He ain't ready. That boy just ain't ready," was all Aunt Brenda said, and she only said it once, all the way home. WDAS blared from the speakers, and Crystelle could feel her spirit nodding to the beat in the back seat.

When they parked on Frazier Street, Crystelle saw Hamp's old, white BMW right away. The same one he'd had in college, when Crystelle had to ride the bus shuttles to get around campus. She thought about going home in the same minute Aunt Brenda asked her if she wanted to come over. She didn't, but she didn't want to go home either, where Granddaddy must've already let him in. Her spirit stood still on Frazier Street, gazing over at the other side. Crystelle peeped to make sure no one was sitting on the enclosed front porch, tucked her head down, and hustled over to Jimmie's house. Her spirit backed up, following her, looking forward at the white car and the trail Hamp must have made from it to Crystelle's house. Longing.

"Telling me I ain't got the right," Brenda threw her black purse on the plastic-covered couch and walked back to her kitchen. "You heard that, girl?" She called over the sound of water pounding into the sink.

Crystelle could hear the water pressure eased and then directed into a plastic pitcher. She didn't figure on answering Jimmie's mother.

"Telling me I ain't got the right." Brenda walked in with one glass of water and drank it. Then she turned and walked back into the kitchen, refilled her glass, and returned. She took another sip and cut her eyes. Sucked her teeth quick. "You believe that?" Sucked them again, longer. "Humph."

Brenda plopped onto the chair and put her glass on the coffee table magazines, which were piled like a dentist's waiting room table. *Jet* on top of *Ebony*, fanned across the table. Jimmie loved *Jet*. Her spirit giggled.

"What you smiling at, girl?"

"Jimmie."

"Huh?"

"He used to—he used to love him some *Jet*."

Brenda leaned back in her chair and looked at Crystelle. Her lips didn't smile and neither did her eyes. Crystelle looked down at the table, twisted her face away. She couldn't help but smile again. Silence hung empty, waiting to be filled.

"The 'Beauty of the Week.'" The words came out in the very laugh she was trying to hold in.

"Crystelle, what are you talking about, child?"

"Jimmie used to flip straight to the 'Beauty of the Week.'" There was no more laughter, no smile, not a grin.

"Crystelle, you know I just came from seeing—from talkin' to—the boy that shot and killed my son, and you sit here talkin' 'bout the damn Beauty of the Week? Excuse my English, but what the hell is wrong with you?"

For a full minute neither woman spoke. Sixty seconds.

Her spirit leaned over, Crystelle heard the plastic sound, and whispered, 'Mama'd know what to say.'

"Mmm."

"What?" Brenda asked, her voice softer.

"I was gonna say, so, what did you say back? To Manny?"

"I told him I do got the right. I got every right. My son is dead."

"Mmm. So, what did he say?"

"Girl, please, I walked out." Brenda drank half her glass. "That boy ain't ready. Telling me about rights and he's the one in jail." She hunched forward, then stood up, turned. "You want some water?" she called, as she walked away.

"No. Thanks, though." Crystelle could see the roll of flesh giving way into the fullness of her pants, as Brenda walked back and forth. Her body swayed into place, gentle-like.

"I should probably go now."

"Don't." Crystelle looked up into Brenda's face. Brenda's eyes gleamed. "I mean, at least don't go 'cause I snapped a—"

"I gotta go because Hamp is over there."

"Huh?"

"I saw his car. When we pulled up."

"Oh. Well, what's he doin' comin' down here?" It was a question that didn't really want an answer. It was more like a statement. A question meant to be considered, like a statement of almost fact. She stood up and opened her arms. Crystelle stood and fell into them; her spirit fell against her.

"Whoa, girl." Brenda's left foot shifted back to hold the weight. "I never hugged a heavy-skinny woman before," she laughed. Crystelle eased away, but Brenda pressed her arms tight around Crystelle's whole body, pulled in. "Come back."

Crystelle felt her legs, arms, body sinking into Jimmie's mother's flesh.

"Come back tonight. Spend the night here. Matter of fact, don't go yet. I mean, I didn't want to snap like I did. Stay a while now, Crystelle. Spend the night later."

Crystelle opened her eyes, looked up the stairs. Her spirit looked too. Into the dark where Jimmie's room waited. She blinked. Closed her eyes tight. Pressed her lips against Aunt Brenda's ear.

"Okay."

* * * *

Hamp's mother hated where Crystelle grew up. Hated that Crystelle's mother wasn't an AKA or a Delta. Hamp's mother hated that Crystelle wasn't in Jack and Jill. Thought a Link was part of a chain. Hamp thought about his mamma's hate as he circled the block two times, trying to find a parking space that would allow full view of his car from inside Crystelle's house. "What about my grandchildren?" she would ask his sister.

He hated that talk, hated the way his mother and sister would sit at the kitchen table, the sparkle and shine all around them, tapping nails that rarely handled raw food and only cleaned when covered in yellow plastic gloves.

Where would Dad be? Golfing? Working? Just out whenever they talked like that.

He hated. Hated that he was like them, now, circling the block two times.

He'd checked into the Adam's Mark and didn't call home. Now, driving in circles, Hamp planned to go back to the hotel, if Crystelle wasn't there. He wouldn't let Crystelle's mother shift to shut the door on him. He would turn and be halfway down the front steps, before she had a chance to shut the door in his face. He'd considered double parking on the tiny street that was really more like a big alley. Some of the back alleys in Mount Airy were actually bigger than Frazier Street. He knew because he'd dated girls from Mount Airy all through high school. He figured he'd stop in front of Crystelle's house, block the street, and run up to ring the bell. That way if Crystelle wasn't home and her mother started shutting the door faster than he could turn, he'd have the double-parked car as a sign— a silent rebuke to Crystelle's mother, a "Lady I learned all about you a long time ago." He'd circled and parked, though. There was a space, and, in the end, he wanted Crystelle to be home, wanted to propose. Wanted to be let in.

Hamp showed his teeth as the front door cracked open.

"Who's that?" He heard Crystelle's grandfather from the back of the house.

"Hamp!"

"Who?"

"Crystelle's friend!"

Hamp heard all this, wind carrying debris into his open mouth, as the door hung half open. He stood, licked his lips, thought maybe he should step inside, until he finally saw her face.

"Hi, Ms. Brown."

"Hi, Hamp."

"I—"

"Crystelle's not here."

This was his moment to step down, backwards, still smiling, down and away. This was when he was supposed to bid "good-bye" and "please tell Crystelle." Instead he blinked, looked into her face, stopped smiling. She pushed out an almost cough of impatient air. "Well, I'll tell her—" she was closing the door when Crystelle's grandfather stepped up and pulled it open all the way. Crystelle's mother's eyes widened as her father pushed her aside without touching her at all.

"Hey, man." He stood back, turned his body sideways, even lifted his arm a little to let Hamp in, as Crystelle's mother walked back into the kitchen. Hamp crossed the threshold, and the dense musk of time filled his nostrils.

"Yeah, man, take a seat." Mr. Brown tipped into the living room. "Got the Eagles on for you." He sat down in a plaid La-Z-Boy as Hamp eased into the couch. They watched the screen, silently, until a commercial came on. "Hey, man, you want a beer?"

"No, thank you, sir."

"Sir?"

Hamp smiled and bobbed his head like laughter.

"When did you start calling me sir?"

"I, uh, Mr. Brown."

"Humph. I'ma Cole, man. My daughters are Browns."

The game came back on, and the men fell silent again, then talked to the screen until halftime.

"Opal, bring out some chips. And something to drink."

"I never knew Crystelle's mother's name was Opal."

"Yeah, man." Granddaddy pulled the La-Z-Boy out of recline, shifted up on the edge of the chair, both elbows on knees, interlocked his fingers, and looked Hamp in the eye. "Both my girls are precious."

The men held eyes in the beat it took for Ms. Brown to walk into the living room with a tray.

"Thank you, Opal," Mr. Cole said, still looking at Hamp.

"Thank you, Ms. Brown," Hamp said, looking up at her, and away.

"Speaking of names, my first one's James." Crystelle's grandfather threw food in his mouth. "So you can call me Mr. James." He swallowed, leaned back, held his beer on his knee.

"Wasn't the boy across the street named James?"

Crystelle's mother looked at her father, who looked at Hamp. Hamp looked back and forth at them both. "You know about Jimmie?" she asked.

"Not much."

"Humph, well, they called him Jimmie, named for his father, who most of the kids called . . . well now, Opal, they just called J what?"

"Mr. J," she stood up as she talked. "Or just Jimmie's father. He's always working—the kids never saw him much anyhow." She walked back into her kitchen without saying anything else.

"Hard working man—still is. Shame."

Hamp considered asking more, thought about almost prying. The quiet went from comfortable to awkward before he could figure the space in the conversation was left for him to fill. By then, it felt too late to ask about a dead boy. Hamp leaned toward the tray instead. "Guess I'll have that beer."

"Humph."

"Do you know when Crystelle's coming back?"

"Naw. Speaking of names though," Mr. Cole took a swallow of beer, "how'd you get yours, Hemp? That your street name or something?"

Hamp coughed up and then forced back the beer rolling down his throat.

"Watch it, boy. Don't choke and die right here in my living room." Hamp coughed more, wiped his mouth with a white, paper napkin. "At least wait till the game is over before you do all that."

The men laughed together before Hamp answered. "I just, I guess I can't believe . . . all these years . . ." He looked at Mr. James Granddaddy Cole and shook his head. "We still don't have each other's names straight. I mean, I've dated Crystelle since college—going on six years almost. I've hardly ever been down here. You don't know my name. I just got yours . . ." Hamp searched Crystelle's grandfather's face for some sort of sign he wasn't rambling.

"Humph." The old man leaned forward again.

"Mr. James I want to . . ."

"What is it, man?"

"Part of me feels I should just ask Crystelle first . . ." Crystelle's mother leaned against the doorway leading to the kitchen. Hamp saw her mouth open, then close. "But I suspect Crystelle knows my intentions anyway. And she's not here . . ." Hamp shook his head. The third quarter was starting. He gazed at the screen out the right corners of his eyes. Mr. James held the remote up along Hamp's line of vision and pressed mute. Hamp followed the remote as Granddaddy slowly pulled his arm back, rested his elbow on the chair, held the remote in the air by his face.

"Mr. James, I'd like to ask your granddaughter to marry me. And, since she's not here, I'd like to ask what you think of that." Hamp watched Crystelle's mother walk back into the living room and stand with both hands on the back of her father's chair.

"Humph."

"I do feel, however, that before you answer, I need to tell you my name."

Mr. Cole laughed a little—but just a little—and shifted in his chair. Ms. Brown leaned her weight on one side and put her hand on her hip, flipped her hair back from her face.

She started, "Well, I—"

"Well, I think," Mr. James cut in, "that that is really up to Crystelle." He leaned forward. "And I will support my grand-daughter in whatever decision she decides." He raised his bottle, Hamp raised his, the men clinked sound in silence, and drank.

"Well, now, I have a whole lot to say in this." Ms. Brown walked around and sat on one arm of the La-Z-Boy. "A whole lot."

"Well, now, let's listen to the boy for a minute, Opal." Granddaddy put his arm out and looked at the ground in front of his daughter. Then he turned back to the couch. "Why don't you start off telling us your name?"

The men laughed harder than they had since Hamp crossed the threshold.

"It's Hamp, Daddy," Crystelle's mother rolled her eyes at her father. "You know that."

"Hamp."

"Yeah, Daddy, Hamp. Hamp Harris."

"Hamp? Aw, wait a minute. Wait a minute. Don't tell me

you're named after my main man on the vibes." Mr. James nodded toward his crates of albums and winked. "Your daddy must've loved jazz. Or your mamma. One."

"Well, sorta—"

Granddaddy stood up to pull a record out. "Shoot, I know you're all right now. Must be from good people. Named for my man on the vibes. Aw, shoot." The dusty racks fell back against the milk crates with a thump. "Forgot." He sat back down. "Record player's broke. Only the CD player . . ." He shook his head while he spoke. "Can't seem to find myself a brand new record player."

"Oh, I can get you a turntable."

"You can?"

"Yeah, not a record player, but dj's use turntables. We can just hook it up to the system you've got."

"Aw, shucks. Trying to be my main man now." Granddaddy chuckled.

Crystelle's mother had sat back on the couch close to the TV. Its muted images flickered behind her face. Granddaddy caught her glare, settled back in his chair.

"So, Hamp—never will forget it now—where'd you get that name? You play the vibes?"

"My full name is William Lionel Hampton Harris."

"Awwwww shucks."

"Yeah, um, my dad insisted on William. That was my grandfather's name."

"He livin'? Your granddaddy?"

"No, he passed."

"Too bad."

"Yeah, so, my mom hated the name William." Hamp sliced his hands in the air over the coffee table when he said the word. "Hated. She was afraid people would call me Billy or Willy or something."

"Billy. Humph." Granddaddy shifted and settled again.

"Yeah, but Dad hated Hampton. See, Mom liked Hampton. Hampton Harris."

"So she's the jazz lover."

"Well, she loved Hampton. It's funny, my grandfather was the one who wanted the Lionel thrown in."

"Humph. He's the one passed?"

"Yes."

"Too bad."

"Yeah, well, I actually had a great-uncle Lionel. Lionel Harris. He had been killed in World War II."

"Lotta brothers were."

"That's right."

"Emmett Till's father was."

"Really?"

"Oh yeah. Died for the same country that let those white boys get away with killing his only son." Granddaddy pointed the remote in the air to the beat of his words. "The same country."

Hamp took a long drink of beer.

"So go on, Hamp."

"So my dad was calling me William. Mom was calling me Hampton. And my grandfather would call me Lionel—just to bust on them both." Hamp looked off toward the kitchen's dull light. From the time he was born his parents couldn't come to agreement—not even about what to call him. He almost said so out loud. Instead, the quiet house made all the noises in the room.

"Yeah, well, my older sister was always a mini-mom, but at age two, she couldn't pronounce Hampton. She was the one, really." Hamp leaned back so he could swing his face back and forth between Crystelle's family. "Could only get the first syllable out: Hamp. Everyone could agree that was cute. So, they all started calling me Hamp."

"Humph."

"So, you don't really—I mean your name—doesn't really have anything to do with jazz," Crystelle's mother said. She pulled a quick laugh from the air in front of her open lips. "You don't know nothin' about vibes."

"I wouldn't say that," Hamp smiled. "I've done my research, studied a little jazz history in school."

"Up at State College?"

"Yup."

"Humph."

"Yeah, got to hear Lionel Hampton live at a festival or two."

"Oh, OK."

"Sounds a lot like hip hop—"

"Ain't nothin' new, man. The old sounds just layer the new. Lemme tell you this right now." Granddaddy leaned forward on both knees. "Ain't nothin' new goin' on in this world."

* * * *

Crystelle was leaning back against the arm of Brenda's new sofa, eating a bowl of soup. She peeked out the window, past curtains heavy enough to block the winter wind, and listened for the high beep of the car alarm being turned off, felt her heart beat slow. For a good hour she'd been sitting, waiting, hearing water rush through pipes while Brenda took a bath. Then she saw Hamp leave her house, hit his alarm, leave her street. She still sat, waiting for a few good minutes to pass.

"I'll be back, Aunt Brenda."

"Huh?"

Crystelle went halfway upstairs. "I'm going home for a sec. Be right back."

"Well, wait a minute. Are you eating dinner over here?"

"Don't know." Crystelle was pulling on her sweater. "I'll be back, though."

Brenda heard the front door slam before she could pull her bathrobe tight.

Across Frazier Street, noises from the kitchen had taken over the whole house. No one noticed she'd come home. Crystelle slumped onto the couch, shrugged out of her sweater, and held it over her chest like a blanket. The space on the sofa felt warm against her back.

"She wasn't ready for no man when he came along." Granddaddy's voice sounded in her ears. "Probably wasn't ready for school. But if the boy wants to marry her, and she wants to marry him—"

"She don't need no man. She'll be fine regardless of him. Niggas ain't shit any way—"

"Who you talkin to?"

"Daddy, I—"

Crystelle could see her grandfather's face, even though he was on the other side of the house. She knew what he looked like because her mamma shut up. And quick.

"And, better than that, what you talkin' about? This man, that man." Granddaddy walked into the dining room, turned back toward the kitchen, and walked out again with his daughter behind him. "The other man, too. The one man left you? The man standing right here, the man of this house right here, told you don't use that word in this house. Shouldn't use it in the street. Shouldn't even think it—"

"Daddy, please, don't start that again." Mamma turned her body toward Crystelle. "She just got back from Eastern State."

"Humph. Well, it's her father, your only wanna-be husband. What they call it now? Baby's daddy? OK, OK, he ain't shit. But he ain't the only one, Opal. It's other men out here. He ain't the only one." Grandaddy's chair creaked back as he leaned on it from behind. "He ain't the only man out here, Opal. Neither is this one like him. Hamp. For all that, neither am I."

'Where is my Daddy?' Crystelle's spirit called out. Her grandfather's face loomed above her, just across the coffee table. Flesh and spit. Real. Her spirit reached out with both hands, held his cheeks. Felt time slip down skin sagging with experience that made words like the very ones he had just said.

"Hamp came by today." Granddaddy came around from the back of his chair and sat down. "Says he wants to make a Mrs. out of you, Crystelle Clear."

"Crystelle, you don't need to feel pressured by this boy comin' over here talkin' to us before he talked to you." Her mother sat on the arm of Granddaddy's chair.

"It's all right." Crystelle was stretched almost full length, the top of her body angled on the couch and her legs rigid, knees locked in front of her. She felt her teeth grinding, her stomach turn. "I know what Hamp wants. Him wanting to marry me isn't news."

"Well, you do what you want." Granddaddy would have tapped his cane if it had been in his hands.

"Well, now, she needs to do what's best for her, which might not be what she wants."

"Mamma, it's all good. I gotta go back over to Aunt Brenda's now anyway."

"Why?"

"She wants me to help her clean out Jimmie's room."

"Shoulda done that a long time ago," Granddaddy said.

"What now? Uh huh. That's too much, Crystelle. You been with her and supporting her all day today. Enough. You don't need to be goin' through that boy's stuff with her, now. That's just too much. And you don't need to be getting married to some boy we don't even hardly know, when you don't even have yourself established yet. Get your career goin'. Own somethin for you. Why marry now?" Mamma wasn't asking. She was telling.

"Opal, quit guidin' that girl's life, now." Granddaddy raised his voice like a fist. "She's grown."

Granddaddy and Mamma looked at each other on the chair for a moment of nothing, then one started yelling over the other in turns. All about who needs to leave who alone and let them do their own business. Yelling, now standing up. "Look, Daddy" and "No, you look" and "That's my child" and "You my child and that's my grandchild." And yelling some more.

They couldn't hear her. No one could hear her, and her spirit pitched and rocked. Stomped, stood and sat and stood up to stomp again.

"Stop, Mamma." It wasn't her spirit. It was herself. "Stop, Mamma." She felt the words, calm and solid. But they had stopped arguing, were looking at her, wild-eyed and still. Then Crystelle realized she was standing too, the sweater fallen on the floor. Granddaddy put his arm up and out, toward her, but Crystelle shook her head. It was too much.

"She's always telling me what to do, Granddaddy," she sobbed through language that her consciousness had never even allowed her to form into an idea before. Before now.

"Hey, now," Granddaddy moved his hand in the air, moved it up and mostly down. Like he was petting a dog. Trying to calm.

"No, she's always been telling me what to do too." Crystelle shook her head, and her braids flew toward the door, then toward the wall, then fell.

"Crystelle, don't you disrespect your Mamma in this house." Granddaddy looked at Opal. He saw his daughter's eyes, cloudy, like only one time before. The time she'd told him, twenty-four years ago, "Daddy, I got myself into some kinda trouble." Like then. Only then.

"What the heck?" Granddaddy raised both hands, kept them in the air. Hovering.

No one moved, and Crystelle felt her spirit sob. 'Why'd you do what she said?'

"Always been telling me," Crystelle's voice almost growled. Mean and low.

'Why?'

"What to do."

'Why?'

"Why, Mamma?"

'Why?'

"Why?" Louder. "Why, Mamma?" She heard herself yell. "Why'd you make me do it?" The yell pitched to a scream. "Why?" The scream pitched higher and higher. "Why? Why'd you make me do it?" Over and over. "Why? Why'd you make me do it? Why?" Her face wet. "Why'd you make me do it? Why? Why'd you make me do it?"

Then a whisper, her spirit's sobs and her own: "Why?"

Granddaddy swung his body at his daughter, at her in the chair, her face in her hands. "What's she talkin' about, Opal?"

* * * *

Brenda was pulling her keys out of her black purse, when she remembered to turn the gas stove off. She had made enough food for her and Crystelle to eat through the night and still have some left over for James. She grabbed her blue coat and dashed across Frazier Street.

* * * *

No one noticed the front door open. Brenda was standing in the doorway between the porch and the living room when she saw Opal with her face down, Mr. James and Crystelle standing and facing her. She could feel the fight in the air, was about to turn and go home, then decided to open her mouth.

"What's this child talkin' about?" Granddaddy's voice over-powered Aunt Brenda's. Still none of them felt her there. She started backing away, had her hand on the knob, turned the deadbolt to open the front door but fumbled and locked it instead.

"What's she sayin', Opal?"

"I don't even know."

"You do know. You know."

Brenda turned the lock back, opened the door, felt the air shift strong just as she heard Crystelle.

Wind whipped through Brenda's jacket, wrapped around Crystelle's words. "I was pregnant. That's right, Granddaddy. Before I went away. I was pregnant and Mamma took me to the clinic and I—"

The front door slammed, Aunt Brenda walked in the living room, her body locked up again. Stone. Granddaddy, Mamma, and Crystelle swung their heads over, silent. Braids flew, then fell. Frozen.

"And what?" Brenda's voice was so quiet, Crystelle shift-ed forward despite herself. "And you what? Lost it?" Brenda saw Crystelle's face, her eyes lost. "What? Took a piece of my boy out of you and—" She swung her head toward the chair. "What did she do, Opal?" Back to Crystelle. "Got rid of it? Just like that?" Between them both, eyes darting. "Which was it?"

Crystelle's mother stood up with her hands out, reaching for both women—her best friend and her daughter. So close.

"She wasn't hardly ready to care for no baby, Brenda. And you weren't hardly ready to hear about it being there."

Brenda looked at Crystelle, didn't look away from her face, while her whispers and tears fell. "I would've raised it. I would've taken care of my own son's child. You didn't tell me?"

Granddaddy fell into the chair, looked at his grandchild, looked away. "Too soon. I said it was too soon for her to go to school. I tried to tell Opal. Trying to push her forward so hard."

"I was ready. My husband was ready." Spit and snot from Aunt Brenda's face sprayed Crystelle. Then she whispered. "Manny killed my child. You killed my son's child. What did I do to deserve this?"

Granddaddy didn't hear her. "I said it was too soon for her to go to school. I tried to tell Opal." Then he realized, a child. A great grand, he realized, late, closed his mouth.

The silence sucked up everyone's voice, everyone's tears, everyone's thoughts. Sucked up everything and held it. Still.

A great grand. His name and Jimmie's name, too, if it was a boy. Coulda called him James the second after Jimmie, or James the third after J, or James the fourth after himself. Woulda had a piece of all of them in him. Had it all inside Crystelle. "I never knew," he said to no one. To air.

"Crystelle wasn't hardly ready, Daddy." She talked to her father but looked at Brenda, looking at her daughter. Crystelle's mother took another step forward. "I don't know why she, why you're here when she . . . Brenda, it's all done now. It's all past. Brenda, if I could go back—"

"Everybody wants to go back." Brenda swung her body away from Crystelle. Their eyes unlocked. Crystelle felt her spirit try to get back inside her, try to crawl inside her. Away from Brenda's screams and Brenda's cries and Brenda's truth.

"Can't none of ya'll go back for me or my son." Brenda's voice cracked high, like a storm cracks the sky, and Crystelle felt her spirit split, like lightening against a tree. Darkness reached out from the place her spirit was trying to get away from. Darkness reached out with a claw, sharp-tipped, quick. Darkness sucked her in and down.

Sustenance must be sliced or slayed. Sliced or slayed.
Sliced or slayed.

Sustenance must be sliced or slayed. Or plucked. To
perpetuate.

Perfect models roll, sway, swing weaves. Snap.

She was snapped. Or plucked. Perpetuate the self.
Feed. Die. Feed. Cycles.

Cycles swirl. Cycles shift. Still falling in spirals.

Going down.

Chapter Seven

Crystelle heard the stairs creak as her mother climbed. Each step sang a note—high or low, soft or loud. Each greeted the weight of her presence, as she climbed in easy, measured steps. She saw her mother's back, her hair to her shoulders just as she clicked open the pin holding it back. Granddaddy sat in his chair, Aunt Brenda just past him in the dining room.

Crystelle let her arm fall out from under the blanket someone had thrown over her. A summons. Brenda stood up. Crystelle heard Mamma stop at the top of the stairs, her hand holding the wooden railing. Crystelle looked up long enough to see her mother turn, eyes full of pleading. And a sudden sorrow when they looked into Crystelle's eyes, even from that far away. Brenda walked past Granddaddy's chair and sat on the edge of the coffee table. Crystelle looked past her, up at the top of the stairs again, but in the space of time before Brenda sat down, Mamma had disappeared. In the quiet, everyone so still, Crystelle heard her mother's footsteps above her head, walking to the front bedroom, shutting the door. And then, she heard nothing upstairs.

* * * *

No one would see what would happen to Crystelle's mamma upstairs. No one ever saw her. She would sit and so still sit and remember. Crystelle's mamma never cried. She would return to then and think through her decision to take her daughter to the clinic. Her thoughts appeared like a checklist, like thinks to do today, that day: get up, make breakfast, run to the Rite Aid, pick up some groceries, get Daddy out of the house, take money out the savings, catch the bus, fill out forms, tell Crystelle where to sign, wait, walk in with her, talk to the doctor, listen to Crystelle say yes, watch her, watch her daughter, watch her walk away, wrapped in white, walking away, down the long white hall.

Crystelle's own daddy wasn't there. The baby's daddy wasn't there. Daddy couldn't know. She can't depend on no man, can't depend on no one. Used to be a man woulda stayed with a woman, made a family out of what they'd been doin' whenever they got the chance. Them days was over. And Jimmie wasn't hardly comin back from where he was anyway, even with best intentions—that much was sure for sure. Jimmie wasn't never comin' back. Just like Crystelle's own daddy, but more for sure.

*　*　*　*

"You passed out, girl." Brenda held her hand. Looked into her eyes. Crying. Silent, then talking again.

"I never even saw that before." Brenda laughed, as a tear dropped from her nose to her lips, slipped into her mouth. "Never saw nobody outside the hospital just passed out. Here." Brenda took out two tablets and gave them to Crystelle. "These will keep you calm."

Granddaddy was standing over her now too.

"Honey, I—" Brenda twisted just enough to look at Granddaddy standing behind her. He backed up and sat down in his chair. Brenda turned around, squeezed Crystelle's hand, then handed her the glass of water on the coffee table while she spoke. "These are gonna put you to sleep again, honey. But I wanted to tell you this." She took the glass away and put it back on the table. "I wanted to tell you I'm sorry. I just," Brenda looked at the doorway that led outside, then back at Crystelle. "I just wanted to come over here and get you, tell you I had made some dinner for us. I shoulda rung the bell, but ya'll don't ever lock that door right."

"You can always just walk in, Brenda," Granddaddy said. "You don't never need to apologize for walking into this house."

Brenda leaned her chin down toward her right shoulder, the side of her face turned toward Granddaddy behind her for a moment. Then she twisted back and looked full on at Crystelle.

"I just—I was shocked. You know. Shocked and—" Brenda's tears fell onto Crystelle's hand now. Crystelle turned her hand and felt the splashes against her palm. One, two, three, four . . .

"I love you so much, honey. I do. My son. He loved you so much—"

"Take it easy, Brenda. You don't need to say everything now." Granddaddy leaned forward in his chair. "You saying shocked. I never knew, either. I never even knew." Granddaddy looked toward the stairs. "And I know I ain't got the words."

"Well, I know this," Brenda smiled, her lips shut tight, then moving again, "I still want you to come on over. Tomorrow night, maybe. I want you there, Crystelle. If you feel up to it."

* * * *

Crystelle's Mamma heard the voices downstairs but couldn't make out the words. She clutched her bedspread as she leaned forward, hoping to catch something clear in the murmuring sounds. Nothing. They were talking without her. Must be. She felt so alone up there. All those years. Alone. And feeling it so strong now.

Crystelle's Mamma had wished—prayed to God to take the baby out of her body. Only because she was young, and the man that used to come around all the time wasn't around so much anymore. At all. They'd stood together once more, at the city hall office, and that was it. Barely stayed through the dinner after. Never lived as her husband. Never nothing. Never even came around again long enough to get a divorce—set her free. Never came back for that.

She was so depressed while she carried Crystelle. No one called it that then. Said she had the pregnant lady blues. No one used words like depression, and there weren't any places to go and talk. Talking might have been nice. Might have helped. Everyone in the family just talked about her Mamma, who had just passed a year before. "Jewel woulda been so happy to be a grandmother," her aunts would say.

But she also knew from her aunts that there were ways to get rid of a baby. Stuff you could swallow. Ways to throw yourself down and make the baby come out dead. She couldn't remember what to take, how to make it once you got it, when to swallow and how it would make you feel. She couldn't remember which way her own body would have to be thrown. She was so desperate to know how to take back her own body. How to change what she had done to herself.

She had even gone to the free clinic one day instead of going to work. The lady at the desk heard what Opal asked for, a way to make the baby go away, and looked at her big belly comin' out of her can't-afford-maternity-clothes and almost laughed. Gave her a few pamphlets and sent her home. Lost a whole day's pay offa that. Offa ignorance. Then the baby came. And Daddy named her Crystelle. No mamma. No mamma-in-law. Just her and her own father and a couple of old aunts that still lived down south and no money for long distance. Shoot, sometimes no money for the phone at all. All alone. Struggling. And sad. But then Crystelle started doing more than just wail and eat and poop and wail all day. Started to smile. To giggle and crawl. Once she could stand up Opal could begin to see some of herself in this child her father had named. Started to see this child was her—the her that could start all over from the beginning. Do well in high school. Maybe even college. And then the acceptance letter came. A big ol' envelope saying she got in, even before she opened it. What a nice term, she'd thought. Acceptance letter. She was accepted into something new and bright and possible. And Crystelle's mamma knew that envelope came right on time. Children she'd seen grow into almost grown had lost their minds back then. Shootin' and carrying on over sneakers and gold chains and drugs. Every night. Even in DC, the nation's capital—the murder capital— every night someone's child died. And they could talk about us killing us equals genocide all they wanted—she was getting her child the hell outta here. It was too much. The Crack Era.

And then Jimmie died too. Seemed like then she knew, her daughter was her all over again, losing the man she loved to something stronger than he was. To the street. But Crystelle wasn't gonna end up like her. Struggling with a baby, and then maybe another from another man who would leave. Opal remembered her own struggle and didn't wish that for her daughter. All those years, a quarter century, alone. Best years of her life. Gone. Wasn't no man gonna do it to her all over again through her daughter. A dead man at that.

Crystelle's Mamma shook her head no. Naw.

She stood up, wiped her face with a wet washcloth, fanned her chest with a piece of pantyhose cardboard, clipped her hair back in place. Tight.

* * * *

Crystelle closed her eyes, opened them, and saw her mother walking back down the stairs again, slowly, like a child done wrong, looking to get off punishment. Crystelle saw her mother, looked at Brenda looking at her mother, then back at her. She nodded. "Sure, Aunt Brenda. I wanna be there too. Maybe tonight."

"No, honey. Not tonight." Brenda looked back at Crystelle's mother again, then at Crystelle. "You need to be here tonight, I think. Those tablets gonna make you sleep hard, girl. I just wanted to tell you I love you, honey. I love you. I love you."

"I gotta tell you something else." Crystelle waited for Brenda to tell her shush, tell her not to try to talk. Instead, Brenda's eyes dried, she leaned in closer.

"What?"

"The night Jimmie . . . the night of that party, I think—"

Crystelle saw her mother step up the last few steps, look at her, shake her head no.

"What, honey?" Brenda asked.

"I gotta tell this. I think that . . . Manny was trying to dance with me that night. All night. Jimmie saw him. Saw him— Manny—grab my arm. Saw me pull away from him, but Manny he held me tight and Jimmie," Crystelle saw Brenda's eyes fill again, "Jimmie, he pushed him off of me, away. They were fighting in the basement, but someone broke it up, and then we were all outside, and I was coming up the stairs, and then I heard this *pop pop pop* and I ran . . ." Crystelle felt the sleep coming to claim her. "I ran, but it was . . . it was because of me . . ."

"Shush, honey."

There it was. Brenda was smiling and soft and kissing her forehead.

"I know all about that night, honey. I found out all about it before I even left the hospital that night. Kept hearing more, even way after the funeral. Heard everybody's version but yours. I was always satisfied to know what happened at the party that night. It wasn't because of you. That was because of Manny and them. And that it was just Jimmie's time. The Lord's time."

Crystelle could hear Brenda talk about loving her and being sorry and wishing she hadn't yelled. She heard it was all right. She heard forgive. She heard secrets. Just the word: secrets. And forgive. Then she saw Brenda stand and look at Mamma. She couldn't hear them talking, but she could see them standing, then holding hands and standing, then holding each other close. Crystelle saw all this as she fell back, headlong, into the darkness again.

* * * *

Crystelle lay in the place between dark and light. Light ahead of her, if she opened her eyes. Dark behind, in the deep sleep she felt fading away. Granddaddy was still sitting on the La-Z-Boy, reclined. His snores were even and Crystelle started counting them, even before she opened her eyes. Inhale one. Exhale one. Inhale two. Exhale two. Inhale . . .

"Talk to me about them ghosts, girl."

Crystelle rolled her head against the pillow, felt her Mamma must be still sleeping upstairs, and looked into her grandfather's face. "How'd you know I was awake?"

"Talk to me, Crystelle Clear."

She didn't have to pee. She didn't want water. She sighed. "Jimmie's been comin' to me, Granddaddy. He's been comin' to me all the time now." Crystelle paused, kept going. "It didn't start right away. I wasn't sleeping much, but I didn't see him.

Didn't dream or nothin'." Granddaddy leaned forward, pushed the La-Z-Boy in, then leaned back again. "I remembered something you told me once. Something 'bout Big Mamma putting a glass of water and a—"

"You did that?"

"Yeah."

"Humph."

"I wrote him a letter, Granddaddy. I missed him. So much. I wrote him a letter. Put it under my bed in the dorm." She looked into the space above her grandfather's head. "And he came. He came and he came and he came." She looked back at his face, at his mouth not moving. "He came when I slept in my room. When I slept at Hamp's, he never came. I slept there. Heavy. In my dorm, I'd wake up tired."

Mamma came down the steps, felt Crystelle's forehead, sat in the corner of the couch. Listened.

Crystelle talked and talked. She told them how the beginning was hazy, brief, and infrequent. How when she studied or sat in class she could focus, but at parties, at anything social, she would drift. She didn't want to go out, and Hamp didn't try to make her. It worked. He could hang out, pledge, party. She could study, be there when he came back to her room. Called her over to his. She talked them through all four years of college—the part of her life they had never seen. She talked all the way up to graduation. The day her parents and Hamp's parents met for the first time, said hello, chatted, took a picture, then went their separate ways.

Crystelle stopped talking and put her hand on the bottle of pills Brenda had brought over, then a new bottle, next to them.

"Forget these," the back of Mamma's fingers pushed Brenda's bottle away. "I want you to take those, the ones you got in your hand." Crystelle looked at the words on the label, counted letters.

"What are they?"

"You lookin' right at it, girl. It's iron pills. Take them, every-day."

"How many?"

"Just one a day, Crystelle."

"No, how many are in the jar?"

Mamma and Granddaddy exchanged looks. Crystelle felt them looking at each other, wondering about her, and put the bottle down.

"So, talk to us some more, Crystelle Clear," Granddaddy said. "What you carrying?"

"You still say I'm walking heavy, Granddaddy?"

"Humph."

"He's coming all the time now, more and more."

"Every night?"

"All night. I can talk to him, I can smell him, I can almost touch him."

Mamma sighed and looked at Granddaddy. "Look," she said. "That ain't real, Crystelle. It's just dreams. You need to quit thinking about that boy, let it go. You got your mind all caught up in more'n five years ago."

Crystelle pulled the blanket up to her chin, turned on her side, reached her hand under the blanket up to her cheek, felt her spirit whisper. 'It is real.'

"It is real."

"Oh, it's real all right," Grandaddy's voice, heavy and deep, demanded. "Oh yeah. I guess you just got the spirit in you, girl. Like my Mamma. Lemme tell you somethin' right now. That snap crackle pop in the corner?" Granddaddy pointed off to the side so strong, Mamma and Crystelle both looked over, then back at him. "That's human form, wishing it were real."

"Daddy, please."

"Hey, lemme tell you. Crystelle." Granddaddy paused, and

his shut lips moved, like he was smacking gums behind them, or chewing on gums. But Granddaddy had all his teeth. Crystelle had never seen him do that before. "Crystelle," he said again. "You were born in the heat of 1968. I saw steam rising from the sidewalk the day you were born. Swear I did. Steam was rising when I got the call about your Mamma—and you." He moved his lips again, just quick, before he spoke again. "Oh, yeah, it's inherited. Oh, yeah. I was sitting out here on this porch, thinking about my own Mamma, when Opal had the nurse call home. Some of us got the ways in us to see things others can't. Like my Mamma did. And I say," Granddaddy looked full-on at his granddaughter, "keep the steam comin' on, girl. Keep the steam comin on."

Mamma sighed. "Well, maybe she needs a reader or something. I can call—"

"She don't need that, bringing all that other energy in here."

"Daddy, I'm trying to work with what you're saying here."

"Look, Opal, you're right. She just has to let that boy go. Let him go tonight, Crystelle. But you got it in you to see things. Ain't no other person gonna be able to sweep that power out the door."

Granddaddy got up to go upstairs. "I'ma be right back."

When Mamma heard the bathroom door close, she turned to look at Crystelle. "Listen to me, girl. You just got yourself all tangled up in what happened to someone else. I know you were there, honey, but you weren't shot. You gotta keep on with living, with your life. That's why I told you . . . you had a full scholarship. A chance. You loved Jimmie, yeah. We all did. But he's gone now, honey. And you're still here. Look, the shooting wasn't your fault, the abortion . . . nothin' that came later wasn't your fault."

'That's a double negative,' her spirit said, giggled.

"Listen to me, honey. You can't control what happened to

Jimmie. Just like you can't control who you love. Or who loves you. But you can control school, work—"

"Humph. That ain't right." Granddaddy was walking back downstairs. "Thought we could control a whole lot a things. Like all of us moving North. Called the Great Migration, but it wasn't all that great." Granddaddy chuckled as he fell back in his chair. "We could leave, but we didn't know for sure what to. But, now, had ya asked me then, I woulda told you what to. Like I knew."

"I'm saying, Daddy. She can make choices, make decisions about things, make the ride easier."

"Well, why'd you make the choice for her, then?"

Everyone knew what Granddaddy was talking about. Mamma had just said the word out loud.

'Why?'

"To enjoy college." Mamma leaned forward a little to look at her father.

"Humph." Granddaddy turned his face toward Crystelle's, kept his eyes locked with Opal's. "Well, did you?"

Crystelle didn't say anything. Thought of ways to count silence. Couldn't.

'One, Mississippi. Two, Mississippi. Three, Mississippi. Four . . .'

"Look, Opal, you are so caught up in what didn't happen in your own life, you trying to make all that happen for Crystelle." Granddaddy's lips moved again, soundlessly, before he could continue. "You try to be so strong."

Then Crystelle could see all that she hadn't seen before. At the burial. An image of herself she hadn't seen before came to her out of the sound of Granddaddy's words: She tasted the dirt. Graveyard dirt. Had thrown herself on the ground. Screaming. Threw herself down and around on the ground. Screaming. No one could touch her. Not for a long time.

'One whole minute.'

She rolled and screamed and reached and tasted dirt, grave-yard dirt that had been shoveled out and thrown around Jim-mie's open grave. She rolled and screamed and tasted dirt until Mamma had grabbed her collar, pulled her head and shoulders up off the ground, and smacked her face. Hard. She'd stopped rolling in the dirt after that. After the smack she'd stopped, cried, felt her Mamma hold her, rock her, love her tight back into the folding chair. Back to the front row. Back to her seat. You have to be strong. Mamma had whispered that, holding her, eyes looking at everyone else looking at her, shaking their heads. Crying.

Later. Later that night, when they were home and getting ready for bed, to go to sleep, Mamma had come in her room, checked in on her one last time. Rubbed her back. Then she'd said this: "I'll never get those stains out, girl. All that cheap lip-stick from everyone all over you was bad enough. Knew that would be tough, even when we were at the funeral parlor."

'She was thinking about that then?'

"But that dirt. All that dirt smudged into all that make-up." Mamma had kept talking, just when Crystelle was going off to sleep. "Look, Crystelle. I know you were upset, but this ain't no free show over here. Don't act all crazy and wild like that again, you hear? Control yourself." And Crystelle had nodded. She remembered nodding and saying, "Yes Mamma."

'Yes, Mamma.'

Crystelle could feel her mother looking, though not at her. At her father.

"Always thought we might be able to move back some day. Back to the same land even, if we could just make enough up here. Always wanted to get back home. Gave that up a long time ago. Thought about it again and gave it up one last time when you moved to New York."

"Did you?" Crystelle asked and looked at her grandfather until he looked away.

"Well, look," Mamma said, "whether this thing you keep seeing is real or whether it ain't, you got to let it go."

"Now, that is sure some truth."

'Like if I dream I die, then I die in real life, never wake up, die in my sleep?'

"Yeah, Crystelle," Granddaddy leaned forward again. "Quit conjuring that boy. Let him go. Now, when you get back to New York, I want you to break that glass under your bed and burn the paper away. That boy Hamp gonna drive you home?"

Crystelle nodded.

"Let him sleep over then. Keep him close for a while. Figure out who he is, when you ain't cheating on him." Granddaddy laughed, stood up. "Been cheatin' on the poor boy with a ghost." Granddaddy chuckled all the way into the kitchen.

'And quit countin' every little thing. Mamma said it anyway. That Miss Michelle, she never could count anyway.'

"Blues ain't about being sad. People say that all the time, but they wrong. Blues is about the totality of life. All of it. Together. Now, the old folks, they had to mask a lot. Humph. Had to mask everything. All the pieces of themselves they wanted to hold onto. Had to hide it underneath somethin' else. Like words underneath the music in a song. Had to make like one thing was another, when it really was the third. Had to or they'd die. That's 'cause a slavery. And that's sad. But, see, they kept it, all them things that make us us. Folk kept it enough so we still here. We're still here. That's joy. And so the blues is all of that. Together.

You understand boy?"

"I think I got it."

"Humph."

—Granddaddy talking to Hamp

Chapter Eight

Mamma stood up to turn on the overhead light in the kitchen. "You should get on across before it gets too dark—too late."

Granddaddy was seasoning meat, and Crystelle was sitting at the table holding Jibri. Shelley sat on a stool in the corner.

"Crystelle Clear."

"Yeah, Granddaddy?"

"What'd Brenda write to that parole board?"

"Don't know. She says he ain't ready."

"Humph. Shame."

"Manny was always a mess," Shelley watched Crystelle shift Jibri on her lap, watched his eyes softly close.

"Well, his brother is worse than ever." Granddaddy put the steaks on top of the stove. "Ever since he came back from the Gulf. That boy was too much when he left, then he came back even crazier. Wild for the night. Saw him beatin' some girl out here on Frazier Street. Remember that, Opal? Had to call 911 on that fool. Humph. Shame."

"I remember that," Shelley said.

Mamma looked at the second hand tick against the wall clock above her head. "You need to get that boy to bed soon, Shelley."

"Boy fightin' so many wars. Still fightin'." Granddaddy was talking mostly to himself, though everyone could hear him.

Mamma knew Shelley knew somethin' had gone down last night. She'd heard Crystelle talking to her on the telephone earlier. But Shelley didn't know everything. Hadn't heard what happened five years ago, and she didn't need to. Mamma also knew Granddaddy wouldn't care who heard what in his house, otherwise he wouldn't have let them in. Mamma did care, and she wanted Crystelle to care, too. Brenda would keep her mouth shut. Maybe not even tell James. That much Mamma knew. She could count on Crystelle to keep quiet too. But her father.

Mamma pushed her chair back and reached up into a cabinet for the tin foil. She pulled, tore, and handed a sheet to her father to put over the steaks.

The thin sheet almost captured a face that Shelley could see from the stool—Crystelle's mamma's frown, twisted in the creases and folds.

"Here, Daddy, that meat looks seasoned to me."

"Naw, now." Granddaddy took the sheet and swung his body toward Crystelle. The aluminum waved and then just hung there, and Shelley could see the shadow of Crystelle's face, a blur from so far away.

"Daddy, I—"

"Sit on down, Opal. I got somethin' to say and don't care who hear me."

Crystelle's mamma didn't sit down, but she didn't say anything else either.

"See, 'cause you got that girl doin' the same thing. It's the same thing, Opal. Just different. You got that girl fightin' in the last war, winning the last war for you. You got her fightin' and winnin' your war, but it's over, Opal. Past. Done."

"Huh?" Mamma laughed with a kind of smirk. "Daddy you ain't makin' no kinda sense right now."

Granddaddy looked at Opal full-on for a minute. Just looked full on till his daughter looked away. Then he turned his glare to Crystelle, softened his eyes, spoke clear. "Don't let her tell you you gotta work twice as hard for half as much. Don't let her tell you that. Life ain't hard. Ain't got to be no more. You got to work twice as hard. Life is hard. Your body is evil. Telling your child to get the switch." Granddaddy looked back at his daughter. "Like you the massa." He cocked his head toward his granddaughter. "They the slave." Then he looked back at Crystelle. "It's all over with. It's done." Grandaddy put the aluminum over his seasoned meat.

"Oh, I know what you're talkin' about, Mr. James," Shelley burst some words out of her mouth without even thinking. Like the words were coming without any real thought at all. "I heard this woman—some woman from some college out on the West Coast, she was speaking down at Temple one night, talking about how we never had no mass therapy session, as a people. Just for the Middle Passage alone, you know?"

"Humph," Granddaddy nodded his head, raised his hand like he had caught the spirit, waved it in the direction of Shelley's words, then stepped back and used the same hand to hold himself up against the kitchen counter.

"Yeah," Shelley said, "I remember her talking, like almost like she was talkin' straight at me, you know. She was saying, and I almost cried, she was sayin' how back in slavery, like, say the master walked by and saw a little child, like a little boy, and said, 'hey now, your boy sure is doin' so well, growing up so well,' you know. Now, the slave woman isn't gonna say, 'why thank you, massa suh, I sure is proud.' "

"Naw she ain't either. Humph."

"She gonna say, 'Him? That one over there? Naw, suh, he a mess. And stupid too. Can't do nothin' right. Ain't right in the head.' "

"Course she is."

"And the lady that was talkin', she asked the crowd, asked,

'now why would a mother do that?' And, girl," Shelley looked at Crystelle, "I didn't know the answer, but I could feel somethin', somethin' strong and strange and embarrassing inside of me just then. And the lady said, and she said it just like this, she said, 'cause she don't want her child sold away from her.' Girl, I just kinda lost it a little right there, and I did feel a tear or two roll down my cheek, but I didn't care then."

"Lemme tell you, we are the children of those who chose to survive. It was a choice. A decision."

"Yup, Mr. James, she said something like that, too. Same thing, really. But I was crying 'cause I was pregnant, you know, and she seemed to be talking right to me when she said we can't do that no more. That those things we did to try to survive as family, as a people, we can't do that no more."

"Like gettin' a switch."

"Yeah, like getting a switch, like we gonna whip our own child like—"

"We the massa and they the slave."

"Yeah, she said that. And, you know, she got to talkin' about how slave mothers would tell their daughters as young as age ten, if they still had 'em, that 'baby, you will get raped, that's a fact, and this is what you got to do when it happen. You can't call out. You can't yell or scream. You got to let yourself go, go someplace far away from where your body got to be. Don't move too much, not to the left or the right, 'cause then it'll just hurt more.' They'd tell 'em that. Preparing them. 'It's gonna hurt.'"

"Sure. Had to."

"Yup. And then, get this, then they'd say, 'and you can't tell.' Can't tell no one. Can't tell no one. Can't tell Daddy—if the Daddy still there—can't tell him, 'cause he can't do nothin'."

"Can't do nothin'."

"Nothin', except get himself killed."

"Killed one way or the other way, but dying for sure."

"Yeah, Mr. James, she said all that, and I looked around and I saw other folk were cryin', too. Crying hard. Not just a tear, like a couple of girls was boo hooin'. And I said to myself, 'what their mothers tell them?'"

"What we need to let go of."

"Yeah, Mr. James. She said we got to let go of the very things that made so much sense during slavery. The stuff that helped us, made it so we could—"

"Survive. Still be here right now."

"Yeah. She said the old rules no longer apply, though they made sense then."

"Logical. Don't want your child sold, say he's stupid. Don't praise him, never make him stand out like he could be worth somethin'. Tell your daughter to expect her body to feel that kinda pain, then tell her she have to shut up about it, can't tell, 'cause can't nobody do nothin' no way."

"Yeah. And, like I said, I was pregnant then. I knew for sure I was." Shelley looked at Crystelle. "You know." Then she looked back at no one in particular. "That's when I knew. I just dropped for the next semester. Had my baby. Took care of me. Shoot. I'ma have my session."

There was a silence after that. Everyone looked down, away from the faces in the kitchen that night, like they were looking somewhere else entirely away from that kitchen. Like they were looking inside.

"Yeah, well," Crystelle said, "you can't just forget."

Granddaddy leaned up from the kitchen counter and stood in the middle of the floor. "Forget? Who said anything about forgettin'? Seem like this whole conversation been 'bout remembering. Don't put words in my mouth, girl. Ain't nobody told you to forget nothin'. Shoot. Like this, now stay with me, now, like this: Always remember the recipe for chitlins. We here 'cause of that. Same time, though, don't allow no swine in this house, sure not no pig guts. My ancestors didn't eat no swine before they got over here. Got stuck." Granddaddy picked up his cane. Tapped it. "Won't eat pig, 'cause I ain't no slave." Tapped it again. "Same time, won't forget the recipe, 'cause once, time not so long ago, I was a slave."

Granddaddy reached down to kiss Crystelle on the top of her head. On her soft spot. "See you tomorrow then?"

"See you tomorrow."

Granddaddy waved his hand in the air and tapped the wall leading into the dining room as he walked away, then upstairs.

Crystelle sat a while longer before she stood, handed Jibri to Shelley, and stretched. She shook a carton of juice, and a braid or two fell forward against her face. No one said anything until Shelley talked about getting Jibri home and to bed. Crystelle walked her to the front stoop and watched Shelley walk down Frazier Street, climb her own front steps, wave, blow a kiss, laugh, and walk inside.

When Crystelle came back to the kitchen, Mamma had just started stirring the rice. Then she reached out, ran her hand down her daughter's head, along her hair.

"Your hair looks nice."

"I was wondering when you'd notice."

Mamma cocked her head to the side and smiled. "Maybe because I always think of you with braids. Braids and beads."

Crystelle laughed into her glass. "That was a 70s thing."

"And early 80s."

"Late 70s into the 80s."

"Whenever." Mamma leaned against the counter next to the stove, looking at Crystelle and stirred, "It was your thing. Now, no more beads. I liked them too. You used to like them."

"I guess."

"Your hair used to chant." Crystelle stopped drinking and

raised her eyebrows at her mother. "Yes it did. Chant or drum or make music or whatever you want to call it, but you definitely sang out to the world with those beads."

"Must have been a quiet world to hear a few clicks in my hair."

"No." Mamma stopped stirring and looked out the window to the back alley. "Ya'll were just loud children. You had loud hair and Jimmie had a loud mouth."

"Maybe we were in competition."

"Ya'll were in sync."

"In tune with each other."

Mamma laughed, "Yeah, ya'll were in tune."

Crystelle followed her mother's line of vision out the back alley, then they looked at each other. Then, they looked away. Crystelle finished her juice, and Mamma finished stirring the rice. Crystelle rinsed her glass, stood looking at her mother. "Well, now I don't have beads, and Jimmie doesn't have a voice." Mamma opened the oven door to flip the steaks, felt the heat against her face. "Mamma? Mamma, can I wear your brown jacket over there?"

"MmHm."

"All right. Thanks. I'll see you later."

Mamma closed the oven door and straightened up. Crystelle went to get the brown jacket, and her mother followed her out to the living room.

"Crystelle?"

"Yeah?"

"Everybody has a voice, no matter what. It's up to us to listen out."

"For a voice?"

"For his echo."

Crystelle buttoned up the jacket. "What if I don't hear it?"

"Then you're lying."

"What's he going to say to me?"

"Say to you?"

Crystelle looked down.

"Say to you? Crystelle, an echo ain't nothin' but the sound you already heard before. That boy can't tell you nothin' new. I told you—"

"All right, Mamma." Crystelle started walking to the door.

"Crystelle."

"Yeah?"

"You're a woman now. Even if Jimmie could speak from his rest, remember he passed when he was still a boy. You can remember what he said to you. You can listen with the ears of a woman grown. But, Jimmie will never speak to you man-like, honey. That chance was mixed with his blood when it fell to the street."

"You mean when he fell to the street."

"I know what I mean. Do you?"

"I don't know." Crystelle looked out the window and across.

"Then you don't."

"Huh?"

Mamma sighed and shifted her weight in the room. "If you don't know, then you don't know."

"I don't know what I mean or want to hear or whatever."

"Girl, you go on to Brenda's. You ain't losing your mind in here."

Crystelle opened her mouth.

"Go on. Go on and get your head straight. You and Brenda need to put that stuff away. Put it all away somewhere. Take a little, throw out some. Put the rest away."

"Where'd you put it?"

"A trunk. So I can open it up and look at it every blue moon."

"Is the moon blue tonight?"

"I don't know. I didn't see the moon this afternoon. Go on, now. I'm gonna burn your grandfather's dinner."

It took a long time for Brenda to get to the door. Crystelle looked up at the sky, but it was full of light clouds. A pigeon rose and fell, then almost disappeared in the twilight.

"Hey, Aunt Brenda."

"Hey, girl. Did you eat?"

"I'm not hungry."

"I have some beans and rice in a pot on the stove."

"Oh, I'll have some beans and rice."

"I thought so."

Crystelle walked quickly through the dining room, looked straight ahead. With a bowl and spoon in her hands, she walked quickly back, blinked, then blinked again, her eyelids closed longer and still.

"Come on, you can eat it up here." Brenda waved from the staircase. Crystelle opened her eyes again. She looked at her mother's jacket across the couch, then over to the top of the TV. Jimmie smiled back at her. She took a spoonful of food, chewed, swallowed, turned, and climbed. None of the steps sang out for her. She took another bite halfway up and stopped to chew. She strained her ears and thought she heard a cackle and words that even the talker knew the intended listener would never be able to hear. She was about to turn around and open the front door, then she remembered the hock and spit. She swallowed the food everyone was making for her, to put some meat on her bones. Her steps were slow and regular now.

"I guess you should finish eating before we start working," Brenda called out. "Come on in the middle room." Crystelle stood in the doorway, not chewing. "Girl, you forgot a drink. You want an iced tea? Huh? Lemme get you an iced tea."

Brenda brushed past Crystelle. "Go on and sit down. There's room on the couch." Crystelle walked in and took a step or two, as Brenda bounded down.

A photo album lay open on the table. She could see herself, people from high school, and Jimmie from where she stood. Spiral notebooks with class of '86 written across the top cover—a three ring binder covered with black magic marker. Tags and images she'd sometimes seen Jimmie make. A few school letters were tossed on the couch. And a trophy. And a few certificates. She saw the yellowed papers from where she stood. The letterhead scattered in a corner on the couch: Penn State, Morehouse, Howard. She never knew he applied to schools down South. She never knew that. She sat down, just reading the first line on each: "We are pleased. . . . We are pleased . . . however . . ." She saw a tuxedo rental slip and took another bite of Aunt Brenda's food. She remembered the year-book; she had brought it home for Aunt Brenda. There weren't any autographs as she flipped through. There was a picture of her and Jimmie. She stopped easily on the page. She stopped easily on that page, even as she took another spoonful from the bowl. Voted best couple. She could think back and remember almost fighting Sheri the day the superlative votes came in. Jimmie was still going with Sheri then. Breaking up. Before he had been inside her body, planted himself there. Seeded. It hadn't hardly been Jimmie's first time. She remembered seeing him try to sneak Sheri and all the rest of them out before his parents got home. She knew what his boys would set up for each other when they would hang in somebody's mamma's basement real late. Shelley used to tell her all that stuff.

"Here." Aunt Brenda handed her a glass.

"Thanks." She drank it half down. "You know one time—" Crystelle stopped.

"What?"

"I shouldn't be telling you this stuff." Crystelle took a sip.

"Well, you have to now."

"One time junior year Shelley and I went to Milik's house."

"Who's Milik?"

"This guy from school."

"Oh."

"Jimmie and his boys were in there, you know, with some girls."

Brenda tilted her head down and looked at Crystelle in the eye. "Some hoochies?"

"Aunt Brenda!"

"He could pull some hoochies, Crystelle. They used to call and hang up all the time."

"That's why he got his own phone?"

"I made him pay for it."

"What?" Crystelle breathed in the warm air around her.

"He wasn't gonna tell you it was a hoochie line. And he never really said it to me, of course. I'm pretty sure James would say hey, hey, hey about it."

"Hey, hey, hey?"

"That's how I knew they were talking about hitting it." Crystelle opened her mouth and turned her head in one quick moment. Brenda just rolled her eyes. "They would say hey, hey, hey and stop talking when I walked in the room."

"Uh huh."

"Yeah, I'm glad though. I wouldn't have wanted to be the one telling him how to put a condom on." Crystelle just sat with her eyes open. "Why do you look surprised at eveything I say today? You're the one sneaking up on him at parties."

Crystelle laughed. "It wasn't a party."

"It was a basement with an extra room, then."

"I guess. Me and Shelley went over, 'cause we knew what they were doing."

"Who let you in?"

"Milik's older brother. But, he didn't let us downstairs. Jimmie came running up and practically pushed us out the door."

"What did ya'll do?"

"Just mess with his head a little."

"Good."

"I didn't talk to him for about a week or so. Till he took me—I don't know—to a movie or something."

"You felt like he was messing around on you?"

"No, not then. We didn't. I hadn't—" Crystelle looked at the blank television screen.

"When did you?"

"Senior year. About a month before."

Brenda looked at the screen too. The women sat still a full minute. Or two.

"You know," Brenda looked at Crystelle's face reflected in the TV, then turned to face her. "I shouldn't tell you this—"

Crystelle smiled, "Well you have to tell me now."

Brenda put her hand on Crystelle's leg, the way older female relatives grab a young girl's breasts when they first appear. The way a mamma might slap her daughter's hips when she starts to grow a behind. "The phone calls had stopped coming."

"Yeah?"

"About two months before. He loved you."

"I loved him too."

Brenda sighed. "I know." She looked down at the table, then back up at Crystelle. "You don't see Shennene in here, do you?"

"Sheri."

"Whatever. All those girls crying like they lost their man at Jimmie's funeral."

"Well, in a way they did. You know Jimmie was good about

not messing around with a lot of girls at once. He liked to have just one girl."

"Yeah, but a different one every two months. I told him don't bring them around anymore. It was too much. Too confusing."

"I'm telling you he would sneak them in."

"I know. We know. I used to cuss him out over that. James knew I didn't like that. That's why I was so glad when ya'll got together. Finally." Brenda smiled and held one hand against Crystelle's cheek for a minute. Crystelle felt her eyes grow heavy with the weight of tears not ready to fall. "I knew it would happen, and that ya'll would last. Gimme my grand—"

Crystelle shook against Brenda's hand, felt her eyes overflow.

"When do you think? How long were you pregnant?"

"I don't know. Don't remember. We never did use protection," Crystelle laughed, sniffed, pulled her face away from Brenda's hand, "so I don't know what your husband was so-called teaching him." Crystelle pressed her lips into a smile. "We didn't do it much, Brenda. I was just getting used to it." She laughed and crossed her legs and still felt the tears fall. "To him. To us, really."

"Oh. So, that guy you've been seeing since college—"

"He's been the only one since."

"Oh."

Crystelle flipped a few pages in the photo album. "This is nice, you know." Crystelle smiled. "Being able to talk to you like a woman."

"I told you, Crystelle Clear. I'm thankful for this day."

Crystelle and Brenda sat, talked, and even laughed a little. James came home from work, joined them for a while, then went to bed. Crystelle pointed to each person in each picture in Jimmie's album. She explained them all to Brenda, even the ones she knew Brenda knew. Crystelle talked and talked. Each person they had known Crystelle talked into a memory both women could share together. She pointed out a few more faces in the yearbook, clutched the college letters, stroked the football letters. She talked about Jimmie on the field, rubbed her stomach, talked about Jimmie in class. Brenda lay back. Crystelle lay back too. For a while, they were silent.

"Well, we didn't get any work done."

"What are you trying to get done anyway?"

"I'm gonna have James carry all this furniture down and sell it."

Crystelle sat looking ahead.

"And I'm gonna give his clothes to the Salvation Army."

"All of them?"

"Most. I'll keep a few things. Pack them with his baby clothes. I'm gonna do Jimmie's room over into a kind of office." Crystelle rolled her head against the back of the couch and looked at Brenda. "I got some ideas to start a business on the side, since they been cutting back on my hours. Nurses making more than me, and I'm in there with administration. I can use that time to make some extra money, you know."

"What kind of business?"

"I got a couple of ideas. Like maybe a daycare." Now Brenda rolled her head to look at Crystelle.

"In the house?"

"We could do the basement over."

"You ever worked with kids before?"

"I raised one."

"You know what I mean."

"Well, I would need a small staff. I could get some students in college for teaching and some retired teachers." Crystelle thought of Shelley. "You know I can run a business."

"I know."

"I got years of experience sitting in front of a computer running someone else's."

"What does Uncle James say?"

"I haven't really discussed it with him yet."

"What?"

"With my man, Crystelle, I need to be sure in my whole head first. James will go crazy if he gets all supportive and I quit. I have to be sure with him because he'll be coming home with all the information and applications, and the next thing I know he'll be painting the basement kiddie bright."

"You have to make sure you want it kiddie bright."

"Yes."

"Well, I think you should. Start small, then maybe you'll be able to quit your job, hire some people to help."

"I got enough pension saved that I could roll over to an IRA, you know."

"I could recommend some good companies."

"Good." Brenda started to pile up Jimmie's things. "So, you think I should?"

"Of course." Crystelle didn't help Brenda. She just watched all the images and all the words piled, stacked, smoothed, patted down. "You gonna miss his room, Aunt Brenda?"

"I'll be in it everyday."

"But it'll be different."

"Jimmie's gone, honey. Everything's different." Crystelle watched Brenda carry Jimmie's things into his room. When Brenda came back, she stood over Crystelle. Her hands were on her hips.

"I'm coming," Crystelle whispered.

"You know, Crystelle, sometimes . . . sometimes I think you went off to school too soon and came back too short. Like your grandfather said. I haven't seen you in a while, and I didn't see you much after the funeral. You never made a real good-bye. You never had time to let the feelings pass through you. I know you did good in school, 'cause your mamma showed me the scores. We were proud and all, but I always did wonder how you were feeling with your best friend gone—"

"My future prom date."

"Ya'll went to the prom."

"Junior. We didn't go—I didn't go to the Senior prom."

Brenda put her hand out, and Crystelle took it. Aunt Brenda pulled her up to her feet. "Come on, girl. You got to say good-bye to all that—prom, marriage, having babies—"

The last word came out as an almost whisper. Brenda looked deep into Crystelle's face. Eyes into soul. "I—"

"I'm sorry, Brenda." Crystelle felt her face wet and hot and strained. "I wish I—"

"Stop. It's done. On that," Brenda stressed the that, "your mamma was right."

Crystelle looked at Brenda and wondered if this was the truth, or if this was just the version of truth they would all agree to accept. She thought about the third shadow sitting above her the night she knew she had to come home. She remembered faces distorted in chrome mirror just a few nights ago. She thought about this for a second. But that second lasted no more than a minute. The feeling she felt came fast and left even faster. She sort of followed Aunt Brenda into Jimmie's room. The overhead light was on, but it was still dark, so Brenda turned on the lamp next to Jimmie's bed. It was so small. Compared to her own bed across the street, his was so small. But then Crystelle remembered she had bought that bed special her first summer home from college. She only stayed home one week, but she spent that week on a full-sized bed. She remembered how proud she had felt buying that frame and mattress. It was the first big purchase she'd made on her charge card. The first she had paid off with her internship pay. She looked at the blue blanket folded over brown sheets. The brown headboard—so small. Next to the bed a nightstand held *Sports Illustrated* and *Jet*, the paper wrinkled and stiff-looking, but dusted. 1986. She looked at the basket of papers underneath two drawers. Lotion and a hairbrush still lay on his dresser. And a picture of the two of them—Crystelle and Jimmie sitting on Shelley's steps—stuck out from the mirror.

"I always thought he just stuck that in there when I came over."

"What?"

"That picture there." Crystelle sat down on the bed. Brenda opened each dresser drawer, looked through them, and tossed the clothes into a plastic bag. She tossed piles of men's boxers at Crystelle.

"Hey!"

"Put them in the trash for me, Crystelle. They won't take underclothes."

"Don't nobody want Jimmie's funky old drawers."

"Don't act like you never touched them before."

Crystelle even smiled as she walked with an armload downstairs.

"Bring up a box of trashbags," Brenda called out after her. Crystelle dumped the whites on the floor, as she searched for trash bags. She tossed the pile into one and brought it and the box upstairs. On her way, Crystelle looked over her shoulder once.

"Put that pile there in the trash bag." Brenda was half in Jimmie's closet now, tossing clothes out onto the bed. Crystelle dropped the few raggedy shirts and socks into the trash bag. The things he had worn the most were now being thrown away. The things he had worn the least would go on to someplace else. She sat down to start folding. Cotton sweatsuits, button-down shirts, hoodies, jeans, khakis, a few big corduroys. Straight-leg jeans, polo and rugby shirts, a Member's Only jacket. 1986.

"This boy had more sneakers."

"Do they take tennis shoes at the Salvation Army?"

"They spray them."

"Like bowling shoes?"

"I guess."

"Oh." Crystelle folded a wool sweater.

"You all right?"

"Yeah. This sweater is nice. I remember this. He used to wear this all the time."

"You want it?"

"Oh, no."

"Take what you want." Brenda was bent over, piling up sneakers. "Look at this," she said, as she straightened up. "The original Jordans." She held them up in the air. "Girl, we fought over these. I was not gonna pay all that money for some rubber shoes." Brenda looked at her hand holding her son's triumph. "But I guess I did." She walked down the hallway with the sneakers, put them in the dark of her own bedroom, and came back. Wordlessly.

Soon all his clothes were folded or tossed.

"He really didn't have that much stuff," Crystelle said.

"No, now that his closet is cleaned out. He didn't have any papers, except high school and college stuff."

"What are you going to do with those?"

"Put them in a box. I got a box for his school jacket and his diploma."

"Diploma?"

"The school sent me one."

"I never knew that."

"I got one of those lockers for his papers and stuff."

"What about those magazines?"

"Girl, put them in the trash."

"What about—whoa."

"What?"

"Look at all this."

Crystelle opened the two drawers, both full of papers.

"It's probably just a bunch of girls' numbers. Just put it all back in the drawer. Here." She tossed Crystelle the brush and lotion. "Put these in there too. James can go through all that tomorrow."

"He's off tomorrow?"

"Maybe. Come on." Crystelle and Brenda carried all the bags downstairs. Crystelle put the trash in the back alley, while Brenda piled all the bags with the good clothes by the front door.

Crystelle walked through the kitchen but stopped in the dining room. She saw Brenda sitting on the couch, her face in her hands. Then she heard the hiss. Brenda sat still, unmoving as Crystelle heard the hiss. She didn't move after the hiss, either. Crystelle heard the hiss of plastic, even while Brenda sat still, then looked up at Crystelle. "Why are you standing over there?"

"I was just thinking we should drink some more iced tea."

"All right."

Crystelle saw Aunt Brenda put her head down again. She backed up, then turned to go in the kitchen. She felt the feeling of wanting to turn around but being afraid to. She kept her back straight, and she didn't turn around. The way she could remember hiding under the covers, scared after watching a scary movie, as a child. Afraid to look up over the covers, still, until sleep carried her away from her fears. Lights flickered in the alley out the kitchen door behind her, as she walked back through the dining room.

"Here." She handed Brenda the glass, then just sat it on the table. She fell down next to Aunt Brenda and took a sip. She could hear the gulp of cool brown slide past her throat. "You thirsty?" Crystelle touched the glass and touched Brenda's knee.

"That wasn't so bad." Brenda's head was still in her hands.

"No. I mean—it wasn't. You're right."

"You sure you don't want anything in the bags?" Brenda leaned forward.

"No, I mean yeah—I'm sure. I don't." Crystelle watched Brenda drink. "Thanks for the football letters though."

"You're welcome, Crystelle Clear."

Brenda nearly finished her tea. She looked in the glass a full moment before she talked. "James isn't going to go through those papers."

"Why do you say that?"

"Because he isn't. He's finished with it a long time ago."

"How do you know?"

"Because I know. He'll never get around to going through them. He'll always have some excuse."

Crystelle and Brenda drank their tea and sat in the near silence of the old house.

"Why do you want him to read them anyway?"

"I can't just throw them out."

"'Cause you don't know what might be in there. So, why don't you just go through them?"

"I tried before. Many a time. It's a lot, Crystelle."

"I'll help you." Crystelle pushed forward on the couch. "Come on."

Brenda smiled, finished her tea, and looked through the tall glass. Crystelle drank her tea with her eyes closed, then she took both glasses into the kitchen. She started humming and hummed all the way back to the old steps. Brenda was waiting there for her.

"I hope you're not going to get mad at my son's numbers," Brenda said, as she made her way back up.

"Hey, I had boys calling me too."

"Yeah? You don't think I know it?"

"Just making sure. I didn't want you to think I was just lying around all day waiting for your son to call me."

"Why not? He always did call."

"But, I wasn't waiting."

"I know," Brenda plopped on Jimmie's bed. "If you had been waiting, he never would have called."

Crystelle laughed as she thought about Hamp for a second, and then, a second later, forgot the thought she'd just had.

Brenda watched as Crystelle pulled the top drawer out from the nightstand. She put it on the bed between them, their half-folded legs and bent arms forming an almost circle around the brown box.

Crystelle plunged in deep, swirled the papers around, fingered a tiny slip, felt it's age. Felt her own age too, just then, and pulled the paper out of the box. "Well, these are numbers."

"Uh oh."

"But they're dates, they're dates."

"People he went out with?"

"No, calendar dates. 5/30, 6/7—" Crystelle read all the dates out loud.

"Let me see that."

"They're for his old job schedule, probably," Crystelle said, as she handed the scrap to Brenda.

"You know what this last date is?"

"What?"

"6/13."

"What? I don't know Aunt Brenda." Crystelle took the paper out of Brenda's trembling hand. It was wet now.

Crystelle looked at the date and remembered. She remembered the party, the dark, the red light, the argument, the fight. She remembered the cries in the night. The screams. She remembered her mother holding Jimmie's mother. She saw her grandfather walking toward her, so fast for him then, now that she remembered. Now she heard her name. She walked quickly through the neighbors, through the boys. She walked through them all. She remembered. She heard the breath sucked in quick. She heard sobs. Now.

"Parties. These are dates for parties, Aunt Brenda."

"Ya'll was too damn organized," Brenda laughed against the thick spit building up along her throat, wiped her cheeks. She looked at Crystelle. "You spending the night? We can finish it first thing. I'ma make James help. Tell him to stay home tomorrow."

"Sure."

"After you came yesterday, I thought I could do it myself. Just seeing you and all made me think I could. But, I couldn't. I'm glad you came home. I got all excited when your mamma called me. Said you were coming home. Then I saw you and figured I wouldn't need your help, but I did. And, well, I guess everything really does happen for a reason. So, thanks—"

"It's nothing."

"Oh, no, Crystelle Clear. It's not nothing. It definitely is not no nothing."

Brenda stood up and walked away. "I'ma put extra blankets out in the middle room. It got cold real quick."

"Weather's funny this time of year," Crystelle called out after her, as she looked at the piece of paper, crumpled it, then remembered the trash was gone. She tossed it on top of the nightstand, made a promise to remember to take it out before Brenda could see it tomorrow, thought, then picked it back up and pushed it deep in the pocket of her sweatpants. Crystelle sat for a minute. Just sitting. She could hear Aunt Brenda pulling blankets out of the closet. Heard Uncle James snore once. But she wasn't really listening. She knew Aunt Brenda needed to put all this stuff away. But Crystelle wasn't really thinking.

When she did think, to stand and go, she could feel the slip of paper there. She could actually feel it. As if the pocket wasn't even there, or as if she were the scrap of paper itself. She could feel it. That's all she knew for sure. The air in the room seemed to beat against her. She could feel the air move even with the windows closed. She rose, walked, and looked back once. It looked so empty, and even if she had been able to hear Jimmie's echo right there, she still wouldn't have been able to know what to say back—to listen for. Brenda was not fine. She was not fine. It was not all right. And if they weren't fine now, how could Jimmie be fine?

She could feel the loss and the ache. She couldn't look back and smile. The room was empty, and she couldn't look back and smile, remembering him there. Her hand rested on her stomach. She didn't realize this until she turned, and then moved her hand away to walk to Brenda. Just then, when she turned away from Jimmie's room to walk to Aunt Brenda, just then, she realized her hand had been on her stomach.

Crystelle was still at the threshold, back to Jimmie's room, when Aunt Brenda came forward with the blankets. "Where you sleeping?"

"Huh?"

"I thought you'd be right behind me and you weren't. So, I thought maybe she wants to sleep in here."

"Oh, no. I'll just sleep in the middle room."

"OK. You know the bed might be more comfortable."

"Oh, no. That's all right. I can watch TV till I fall asleep."

"Hey, I'll watch a little with you. You want anything to eat or whatever?"

"No, I don't feel like going downstairs."

"Oh, I'll go—it's no bother."

"Aunt Brenda, you know you don't feel like going all the way back down there either. Let's just relax."

"All right."

It seemed, then, as if time was turning back upon itself. As if, when Crystelle arched her body on the sofa, time too was stretching behind itself. Sleep could overtake her without the outward stretch—she would not need to embrace, to reach for sleep, tonight. The light from the television became enough.

Brenda held the remote and lingered on images that were familiar. They arrived each week in similar form. The same shows. The same characters. The same stories. Almost exact. And she lost the looking over her shoulder feeling until, as always, sleep slipped in between the covers, rocking her off.

She was asleep until she woke up. It was one thing to wake up. It was another to wake up and be transformed. This she embraced. The change was stretched forward to receive, even as her spine still arched backward. Somewhere in the middle, she stood up straight.

Crystelle could feel a whisper. That is what she felt at first—a soft spray of words with no meaning. Another secret she would never be able to tell.

If she stood up, maybe she would fall back asleep. No. She needed to close her eyes right away. That was the only way to drift back off. She laughed as she lay there with her eyes shut too tight. She reached up and then down on herself, longing for Hamp. When she reached her self, she smiled. The longing feeling stopped. She felt warm and sleepy again. Her eyes relaxed and she smiled.

In one instant, a bright light flashed outside of her, outside of the middle room. She opened her eyes wide, lifted her head just a little. Then she heard a deep grumbling. Crystelle lifted her face more, then realized it was all outside the window. She realized all the flash and roll was taking place way past her, and West Philly. Somewhere above the earth itself. The bright light flash and deep thunder roll was happening. It really had nothing to do with her. She felt the pillow again. She let her head roll against the softness.

And then she began to dream. She knew she was dreaming, even though she was in the dream. Even as the dream was taking place, Crystelle knew where she was.

* * * *

The streets were hot. She knew because she was barefoot. She felt the clap and roll. Felt it against her bare skin. Felt it at the nape of her neck, down her spine, along the width of her body. Each new burst of flash and sound resonated in her flesh. She felt her spirit shake.

She sat looking out the window, past paint chips flaked and peeling along the wooden frame, past waves of rainwater against the old glass. Out there, somewhere in the wet alley, she could just see him. A silhouette made real with the flashes of light God saw fit to send down. He was teasing her.

You got to tell . . . You got to tell Mamma to stop. You gotta tell Mamma to just leave my room alone. You got to tell.

"Why don't you tell her yourself, Jimmie? Why you always got to be bothering me all the time?"

Aw, Crystelle. I'm not bothering you. Am I? You know you like me coming to see you like this.

And she did.

Plus, he said smiling, *she won't listen to me no more.*

She heard it again: swish, swish, swish, swish. Steady. She felt herself steady after she first heard the swish. Then she saw them. Rhythm in air on hot asphalt, then back on air. Then she saw more, him. He smiled, and she could feel herself smiling. She rushed forward to meet him again.

Oh how she missed his feeling. When he had his arm on her waist, or both arms holding her close. In the times they'd kissed. He was the first to touch her inside. She could feel his hand again in the dream. She could feel his hand holding her inside, in that place where a boy's hand could be inside and outside at once. Firm. Searching. She felt it as she rushed forward. Her skin against his. Once he had felt her breasts when they were new. They had risen from the bed, together, and Crystelle caught a glimpse of herself in the mirror above his dresser. She could see them together like that as she rushed forward, and she could feel him just holding her inside, just touching her there.

* * * *

Lightening flashed again, and Crystelle opened her eyes. She was standing with a blanket draped over her shoulders, the warm inside feeling gone. She stood alone, in front of Jimmie's mirror.

The back alley was dark and so was his room. She turned on his overhead light and ran her fingers through her braids. No beads. He was still gone. She fell on his bed, pulled his pillow close, smelled stale cold time.

She wrapped the blanket tighter, stood up, brought the other blankets from the middle room, and laid back down on top of the brown spread. Her breath slowly warmed the cold blue pillowcase. Her eyes closed.

Sleep was a place that kept dreaming.

* * * *

Swish, swish, swish, swish. She could feel her body leap and fall. The ropes were tangled in her feet. She looked up. There, looking back and laughing, stood Sheri. She threw her ends of the ropes at Crystelle. They tangled in her braids. Sheri reached down, picked up the ropes, and, laughing, pulled them. They yanked through the braids, through Crystelle's hair. She looked down, hearing laughter still, and watched as her beads fell out onto the street. She looked at the beads as they steamed, burned, melted. They melted onto the black asphalt—each one a tiny spot, red on the street. She could hear Sheri laughing still.

Crystelle looked up as the laughter changed. In the dream haze emerged her mother, younger. She stood, hands on hips, shaking her head. Crystelle looked down again and turned her face, just enough to hear Young Mother. "I told her they shoulda done that boy's room first. I knew it." Then everyone disappeared.

* * * *

Crystelle settled and slept in the warm darkness that doesn't dream, that forgets, for an almost hour. Behind the almost hour, the dream haze blew again.

* * * *

In the dream she was walking again, downstairs, feeling the wall with one hand, holding a blanket with the other. Light from the dining room glowed. Voices, mumbles, bursts of laughter that felt like sighs. The warm glow came from bodies, four, seated at the old wood table. She was looking at herself, herself now, with Jimmie then. 'That's not right,' her spirit whispered in her ear. She shook her head and frowned, saw

Jimmie looking at her sitting and smiled. She shifted feet, about to move forward, when Jimmie put his hand up. The hand stopped her from walking, even though he was still looking at her sitting self in the dream. Jimmie was at the head of the table and Brenda was at the other. She heard James snore in the bedroom above. 'Which James?'

Brenda was smiling at her sitting self too. *I'm happy for this day, Crystelle Clear,* she said. But it was Jimmie's voice. Brenda's mouth was moving, but she heard Jimmie's voice say those words and when she looked at Jimmie again, she saw his lips were moving too. All three looked, in synch, at the fourth chair at the old, brown table. Their eyes blinked, at the same time, and looked over, at the same time, at the only person sitting there whose face Standing Crystelle couldn't see. She shifted to walk forward, to call out, to reach with her hands to see the face of the little person sitting there, but Jimmie's hand snapped up again like a slap on air. Standing Crystelle felt her face. Stood still.

The little person wasn't in a chair at all, it was a high chair. It was a baby. It was a baby in a high chair, and everyone could see the baby but Crystelle standing there. And her spirit. She felt her spirit in the dream, the part of her that had been disconnected so long ago, tip up, walk around the table. No one sitting noticed her spirit there, only Crystelle could see her tip around and look in the face of Jimmie, then Sitting Crystelle, and then Brenda. And then, last, the baby in the high chair. Her spirit lingered, tried to catch the baby's waving hands, tried to wipe the baby's face with her spirit fingers and thumb. But the baby squealed, shifted, shook. "Come back," Crystelle called out, and her spirit tipped, then walked, back to her. 'So beautiful,' her spirit said. 'It's all so beautiful.'

"What does the baby look like?" standing Crystelle asked.

'It's a boy, a big baby boy,' her spirit smiled.

"What does the boy look like?"

'Brown. The baby is brown. And so big.'

"What's the baby look like? Me or Jimmie?"

'Big like Mel.'

"Big like Mel?"

'Big like Mel. And brown.'

"Brown-skinned?"

'Brown like Shelley,' her spirit called, walking upstairs. 'Brown like Shelleeeee,' from the top of the stairs now.

Crystelle looked back at the old, brown table. At the four of them: herself, sitting, and Jimmie, and Jimmie's mamma, and the baby who couldn't turn around. The glow so warm above them all as they laughed. *I'm happy for this day,* Crystelle heard, as she turned to go. *I am so happy for this day.* Crystelle looked back, and Jimmie turned his face to her, winked, and turned back to the baby, to his mother, to herself sitting at the old, brown table. Crystelle ran upstairs. In the dream she ran upstairs, lay back down, shivered, wept.

The dream haze shifted, and Crystelle could feel fingers. They were touching her, and she was moving. When she lay still, the blue sheets still moved and Jimmie laughed, bit her ear with laughter. She jumped when he laughed, but the fingers stayed where they were, only stronger, so Crystelle lay back again and moved again, lying still.

You lookin' so good to me, I had to come get me some.

"Yes."

You lookin just like a Beauty of the Week.

"Yes."

Better not ever pose like that, though.

"Yes."

She lifted one leg up, then the other. She bent her knees,

and her feet were flat by her hips. They arched. Flat again. Jimmie put his hand on her stomach and so did Crystelle. It grew.
The stomach grew and lightening flashed just as she saw Jimmie's smile drift into the dream mist.

* * * *

That's how she knew the dream was over. That's when she sat
up. The light was still on, and Crystelle saw herself alone,
again, before she went back to sleep. She was so exhausted
now. She just wanted to sleep. She wanted the dreams to end.
The mist blew in her sleep, and she tried to wake up. She felt
her spirit shaking her, 'up, up.' But she could not wake up.

* * * *

*Aw, Crystelle, it ain't even worth it. Let's go outside and play in the
snow. Come on, Crystelle, you're always thinking too much.*

"Oh, Jimmie."

*Yeah, but don't even worry about it, Crystelle. 'Cause I'ma be rich.
Yeah I am, too.*

'He's dead,' her spirit whispered, even in the dream.

*Yeah I am. I'ma be an actor, and move out to Hollywood, and have
lots of money, and buy my Mamma a nicer house. And I'ma come back
for you after a while. Dag, Crystelle, give me a couple of years to have
some fun by myself for a change. But I am gonna come back for you,
Crystelle. And we're gonna be rich and married in sunny California.
And all you're gonna have to do is sit around and take care of our house
and our seven kids and just think and sit all day. I'm gonna make it.
I'm gonna make it so you can sit and think all you want, Crystelle. I'm
gonna make it.*

"Oh, Jimmie." Crystelle's forehead leaned against the cold
glass made black by the darkness all around. Her breath fogged

a circle on the pane. The streetlights flickered, sparked on. Everyone was playing double dutch in the snow on Frazier Street.

'Wrong way. And he's dead.'

"Your window faces the back alley."

Aw, Crystelle, you think too much.

"But I know I'm right."

'You are.'

Yeah, but I'm gonna make it so you can look out the window and think all you want. Yes I am too, Crystelle. I'ma make it for you.

Crystelle's weight pushed the window up, and the hawk reached in with his clawed hand, whisked Crystelle and Jimmie outside on wind. She shivered as her friends rolled in the snow. Tara, Shelley, and Michelle. Sheri. Manny and them. Him too. Jimmie and Crystelle ran behind a parked car. Crystelle just crouched down with her head in her hands. Jimmie started a snowball fight. White flakes packed hard and thrown. She could see melted beads against black asphalt against white snow. She shivered. Sheri dropped a big lump of snow on top of Crystelle's head. She licked the grit that turns snow into slush. *You remember that taste.* Jimmie ran after Sheri, then ran back. Manny stood, towering. Laughed. Threw a ball of snow at Jimmie. So hard. Jimmie fell back from the force of the snowball. Fell back. Crystelle turned to pull him up, but his body wouldn't move. Snow fell on his body, on the red soaking through his clothes now.

"Oh, Jimmie."

Crystelle opened her mouth to scream, but just as she turned to cry out, Jimmie reached up, stroked her face, giggled, winked. The red coagulated, formed beads, then melted, soaked again. Jimmie winked another time, ran after Manny, stayed far.

Crystelle turned to chase after him, but Granddaddy stood

over her, threw a Hawkins Funeral Home Great Queens and Kings of Africa calendar at her. 1986. He pointed to the boxes holding the dates in time.

You walking heeaavie, Crystelle Clear.

"You just shut up."

Aw, come on, Crystelle Clear, you know you walking heeaavie.

Crystelle rolled her eyes at Jimmie, then remembered.

"Oh, Jimmie."

Granddaddy tapped the calendar twice, the broad face of a queen, a date, and then, he faded into the dream mist, into the swish swish, into the snow.

Aw, Crystelle.

"Oh, Jimmie."

Here, this is for you. He touched her cheek, so soft, so cold, and handed her a frozen tear.

"Oh, Jimmie."

Come on, Crystelle. Try and catch me!

And she did. She tried to get up in the dream haze. She tried to move. But her stomach was too heavy, too full, it was still big. She couldn't move.

"Oh, Jimmie."

Aw, Crystelle.

"Sit with me."

You don't tell me what to do.

"Yes."

Go on.

"I was born in the heat of 1968. My granddaddy said he saw steam rising from the asphalt the day I was born, and I believed him."

Go on.

"Yes."

Go on.

"That's all."

Go on.

"That's—"

You walking heavieeeee.

"Stop it, Jimmie."

You don't mean that. Here.

He handed her the melted beads. He scooped into the snow, into the black street. *Here.* The palm of his hand held the melted beads, all red and melted into her hand now, as he poured the steaming red red into her own open hand, cupped like she would be drinking soon.

Here.

"Stop it, Jimmie!" The red red burned her hands, burned and steamed right through her hands back onto the street, and he was dead dead again beneath her because she was over him now. "Oh, Jimmie!" Above her the red red kept pouring into him onto her, and her hair clicked in the growing wind. "Oh, Jimmie." She looked down at her own torn shirt and back again. Into his eyes. He opened them.

Heeaavie.

"Jimmie, I thought—"

Aw, Crystelle, stop thinking.

"Yes."

He leaped up and threw her over and reached inside her again.

"Sheri will see us."

Not in here.

Crystelle could feel the sheets cold, then warm where she lay in his bed with him on top of her again. His hand inside, so deep inside, holding her, but outside too. "Oh. Jimmie." He smiled into her face, kissed the salty wet. *Here.* He pulled his hand out from the place that let him inside and there, in his hand, he held her beads. Red red beads. *Here.*

"Oh, Jimmie."

Lo Lo Bia.

"Yes."

Lolobia.

"Lolobia."

Open em, girl.

"Yes."

She threw the beads behind her, and the song they made rolled off into the dream mist too. She could hear them, far away now. Like tiny drums. Like a gourd.

* * * *

When she opened her eyes again the headboard, so small, was knocking, almost finished knocking against the wall. She was soaked. She could feel the moisture and the heat, and she knew she needed to wash, but sleep felt so good because of the dream haze. Outside the blankets was cold and alone in the mirror. Under the blankets, she was closer to him. She closed her eyes.

* * * *

Wanna dance one more time?

"Yes."

Do what I say.

"Yes."

The swish swish swish swish lifted her soul enough for her body to turn and follow the sound her ears remembered. *Let go. Come to me.* The little boy called, dancing, and Crystelle dropped, squatted, feet flat near hips just above touching in the street that steamed beneath her spread legs. She felt her own fingers outside the place where Jimmie had just gone in. *Let go, Crystelle.* The boy called, dancing. But Crystelle couldn't move her cupped hands. *Let go, Crystelle.* But Crystelle wouldn't move her hands. Flowers fell out onto her hands and the street, and she smiled until they wilted and died.

In the dream Crystelle knew she could shake herself awake. In the dream mist she remembered the place she had just left that was real. Then she saw her spirit. Not holding her hand, not whispering in her ear, not looking eye to eye at all. Her spirit was touching and whispering and looking at Jimmie. Jimmie didn't smile. For the first time, he stopped smiling, but he kept dancing. He kept dancing like a mule keeps walking in circles to keep the wheel attached to his body moving. He danced not like a boy she loved, but, in the time her spirit spoke to him, he danced like a farm animal forced to take what came perfectly naturally and make it work. To survive.

Crystelle stayed still, but her spirit let her hear. 'She's not going crazy down here. Mamma said it and Granddaddy said it and your Mamma said it too.' *Didn't.* 'Might as well did for the way she was lookin.' *Aw.* 'It's not fair or even nice any more.' *What you talkin? She likes it.* 'Yeah but look at her now.'

Both looked over at Crystelle now. She saw them as she crouched, spread, so low. But she couldn't hear them anymore. In the dream Crystelle knew she could shake herself awake. In the dream mist she remembered the place she had just left that was real. She looked over her shoulder, still squatting, then looked back. Her spirit wasn't whispering to Jimmie anymore. Jimmie was dancing, and she thought about dancing too. She could dance with him here or sit alone there. So, she decided to rise, slowly, and only her legs were shaking a little.

'We gotta go soon.' Her spirit whispered to her as legs shook. 'Say good-bye. Just give him something. He needs something to cross over. A present. And say good-bye.' Crystelle shook her hair, her braids whirled above her head. 'You wanna stay here forever.' Crystelle stopped shaking her head and listened. 'This ain't right.' Her spirit tipped even closer, cupped her hand over Crystelle's ear, looked behind at Jimmie, then cupped even closer.

'He's dead.'

"Just passed over."

'He's gotta cross all the way over before you could even say that.'

"Huh?"

'Let him cross. He has to cross.' Then her spirit pulled back and looked in her face. 'You wanna live in the park too?' Crystelle looked down. Away. Back at her spirit's self. 'I'ma be over here.' Then her spirit walked into mist behind them both, disappeared. Crystelle reached out with her hand to find her spirit in the mist, but just then Jimmie lifted his hand, too.

Jimmie reached and ran his hand through her braids, pulled off her beads, just a few, and put them in his pocket. *I'ma keep these.*

"Yes."

That all right with you?

"Yes. For you."

They're my present.

"Oh, Jimmie."

You tired?

And she was. All the time.

Me, too. Jimmie smiled again.

He ran his fingers through her braids again—the ones with no beads—and the ends of double dutch rope came in his hand.

He started turning. He was turning the ropes and smiling, and in the dream haze Crystelle remembered. No one was turning the other end of the rope, and, she remembered, Jimmie never played double dutch. He was smiling and turning still so Crystelle forgot about thinking all that and jumped beneath the ropes.

But she was outside the ropes somehow, even though she

had jumped in. On the other side she turned around and slipped under and between and, again, she found herself outside and past their steady swish.

Jump in.

"I can't."

Aw, Crystelle. Just let go. Let go and jump back in.

Crystelle looked at her open hands. She put them high above her head, rocked back and forth, letting her body remember the rhythm, letting her body realign. And then she jumped in. She jumped, facing Jimmie, beads clicking, smiling.

So tired.

She was, but the more she jumped the closer she got to him, so she jumped anyway. She jumped closer and closer to him until, in the dream haze, she was right in front of him, almost touching him. His arms were still out, still turning the ropes, and she was inside them now. She had stopped jumping, and his arms were almost around her.

She stood waiting. In the dream haze she wanted him to take her in his arms, close. She wanted him to kiss her soft. She wanted to feel warm and soft against his body, warm and hard.

Let go and jump back in.

"I am in."

You know what I mean.

And when she looked at her hands one last time, when she saw the palms of her hands one last time in the dream haze, then, she remembered she could. For the first time, she remembered she could. He was still turning the ropes, but she had stopped jumping now. In the dream haze Crystelle stopped smiling. She floated back, away from Jimmie, who was still smiling and still turning the ropes, and she watched all her beads fly away, as her braids waved in front of her in the dream haze. She would never know who was turning the other side of the ropes.

You not heavy no more.

"Oh, Jimmie."

This your spirit's good-bye. And he kissed her, so sweet, like the first time. An almost kiss, really, like the first time their lips ever met when they were both young, both flesh and spit. It was so nice. His face hovered near hers for time Crystelle would never be able to count.

Then, the dream mist blew in so thick, Jimmie became a sound.

You not heavieeeee.

"Go—oh, Jimmie."

Heavieeee.

"Good—Jimmie?"

Crystelle thought she saw him dancing again, but it was the look and whir of red red flowing out in front of her, her facing back in the dream mist, still searching for the dancing boy, dancing away. Then, not searching at all. Just sound.

You not heavieeeee.

"Oh, Jimmie."

You not heavieeeee.

"Good-bye," she called out. But it was only a whisper.

She had to face forward now, the brown and blue were rising up to meet her.

"Good-bye, Jimmie."

Heavieeeeee, meeeeee. Don't forget meeeeeee.

"No. Oh, Jimmie. No."

Don't forget meeeeeee.

Sound rolling so far away, it became just a feeling she could feel back. The feeling was a remembrance. The feeling said good-bye. The brown and blue held her now. She felt the jolt of landing, the inside jump.

And then, she woke up.

Crossed

The room was still dark but lighter. She could hear it. The rush and spray. Water was running through pipes, and rain was falling against glass.

Crystelle felt wetness. She stood up and looked in Jimmie's mirror, alone. She turned and looked behind herself and saw her body had been flowing, too. Crystelle went to the middle room and got her mother's jacket to tie around her waist. Then she went back to Jimmie's room, checked the blankets, folded them. With one last look at the only room left for Brenda to change, Crystelle turned back around and followed the morning sounds. In them, she found the hug and the kiss and the look in eyes she would always remember. In them, she heard another good-bye, felt the movement from room to room to say good-bye. It felt good knowing she could hug Brenda close like that. So close.

Crystelle rushed across Frazier Street. The rain fell and ran along her face and hair. She rushed in and up and into the heat and mist in her own house now. She could stand under water and feel heat and mist too. The dressing and calling and relaxing in soft cocoa butter brown, so soft, so smooth. Her own self. The feeling of her body flowing out red red into the world, that was all a fresh feeling for remembrance. The feeling of hot water and warm clothes and soft brown, of her granddaddy's pancakes, of laughter and talk, and of Hamp returning in the day, that was a feeling so real, Crystelle could touch it. Touch him. She could touch it deep down inside herself. The relief, that was a feeling for remembrance too.

She felt like she had been touched by God. Touched by the sun. In this space where she now felt free, Crystelle knew something miraculous had taken place. She also knew this kind of thing happened everyday. This falling into the pit, clawing at the grave dirt that would suffocate and kill. But there was more underground than just old bones. Crystelle knew that now. And knowing was the everyday miracle.

Knowing Jimmie had been real—spirit real—allowed her to strike a deep well of memory. Dip in. She had dived into the well, taken a last breath of childhood experience, and dove even farther, into the well's waters, to the depths, to the bottom. There she'd found the well was fed by a spring, which she'd also swum, underground. The spring led to a river that flowed like the Nile, up instead of down. This river led to a sea, and she learned the oceans were too deep to swim across, that all the seas splashed into each other, that there could be no land, just swimming around and around and on to forever all around. Until she drowned. But there would be no drowning for Crystelle. Now she stood clean and dry and warm, even as cool air blew in around her. Grave dust washed away. Nails clean. Someone had pulled her to land. She'd lain there gulping, half in, half out, until she caught her breath. Then she had hoisted herself all the way.

She stood on the front steps of her childhood home, looking across at the other side. Her grandfather stood behind her, holding the front door open. Her mother stood behind him.

"The weather's finally shifted," Granddaddy said, as he zipped his jacket, looking at Crystelle.

"We might get another Indian Summer," Mamma said, thinking about the calendar.

"Naw, this is it," Granddaddy promised, pulling Frazier Street's air into his lungs.

Mamma was about to talk back again, but instead she sucked in a little air, too, noiselessly, and picked up her jacket instead. "Come on, Daddy. We gonna get all the driving we can outta this rental car before Crystelle leaves tonight."

When they left and the house was quiet, Crystelle washed the clothes she'd worn all weekend, felt them hot and magnetic coming out of the dryer, and folded them into her overnight bag. She washed her sheets and towels and straightened her room. Just as she brought her bag downstairs and plopped on the sofa in the closed-in porch, Hamp drove up and parked. He saw Crystelle through the glass as he crossed Frazier Street, and Crystelle smiled back.

She sat with him and talked. Crystelle told Hamp everything that had happened. Everything. From before they met to last night and now. She told him her period had come late, that she hadn't been keeping track of her own body's time and had thought she might be pregnant, but now was sure she wasn't. She told him she'd been having dreams about Jimmie, but only that. Almost everything. She told him about Manny and the parole board and how it felt to have grown up with him too. She told him good-bye, at least for a while, because she'd need to be alone. And then, he left. And she smiled. Felt good.

The dream haze was gone, but Jimmie wasn't. He was a feeling for remembrance she could touch without carrying. It was a feeling for inside, not for on top.

The feeling was being able to let love flow inside. The night sound was the sleeping sigh of her breathing and pushing out of herself, the soft drops of herself in the flow. The shadows and whispers were somewhere else now. She was somewhere else and Frazier Street was too, even without them. The flow was inside of her pouring out into a place that was real. So real. She could still see the past and be joyful in time now. She could see herself, in her own rental car, driving back to Brooklyn. She could see alone time, time for Crystelle. Clearly. Her eyes shone at the vision of what would be next. The spirit dance was hers, dancing ahead to see.

Acknowledgments

Thank you, Michele Rubin, for your unwavering enthusiasm and for shared vision, for being so dynamic, so supersmart. Thanks also to Nadia, Talia, and Michael at Writers House. Malaika Adero, an editor and a force. Highly regarded by many. Much admired by me. You make things happen. Thank you, sis. Thanks also to Krishan at Atria.

Thanks to the people of 1238 Hunter West: my colleagues who work in that windowless box, especially Mark Bobrow, a very good reader, and Michael Thomas, a very good writer. Richard Barickman and Kate Parry for the early support. Sylvia Tomasch for the nomination. Cristina Alfar for being there. Elena Georgiou for advice and feng shui. And especially Thom Taylor, who does everything well. Joyce Toney for the sister-hood, Kassem-Ali for the brotherhood, Ehiedu Iwerierbor for the leadership. Thank you, Edey-Rhodes. Thank you, Barbara Saunders. Thank you, Dennis Paoli, for the copies—I got the deal! Thanks to the women and men in the mail room, the computer lab, and duplicating, the ones who truly make the college happen. My students at Hunter College, who let me talk and talk and talk it all out until I was ready to write it down. Just right. Thank you.

Thank you, Kevin Powell, for saying we needed a mass counseling session, just for the Middle Passage alone, when I was listening. Thank you, Gil Noble, for airing Dr. Joy Gruy-Leary on *Like It Is* when I was watching. Thank you to the sister in D.C. who walked past my stoop, talking to her homegirl, when I was sitting. I'll never know your name, but your voice guided me to this story, and I thank you, sister.

Thank you, Ms. Louise Simms, for challenging my thinking and writing and Mr. Ray for insisting on present, active verbs. Thank you, Daphne Dumas, for tea. Thank you, Chi Ogun-yemi, for Black women writers around the world. Thank you, Komozi Woodward. And Regina Arnold—thank you for guiding and insisting and even scolding at times; may you rest in peace.

Thank you, Grace Edwards, for telling me this was a novel when I thought I was writing a collection of short stories. Thank you, Jeffery Renard Allen, for telling me the work was ready to make the rounds. Thank you, Frederick Douglass Creative Arts Center, for being the space to which I could go. And Fred Hudson. You kept telling me to get it done. I did. You live on in the Center, in the words you made happen with your never-ending support. You live on in my eternal gratitude.

Thank you, AJ Verdelle, for your guidance and support at the FAWC. Marie Brown, godmamma to so many of us, thank you. Thank you, Camille Yarbrough, for celebrating the stoop—a basket of love indeed. Thank you, Debrena Jackson Gandy, for the magazine interview that really became a conversation about mothers—about our matrilineal heritage. Thanks to the Frank Silvera Writers' Workshop. Thanks to Howard University for the fine arts minor. Thank you, Brian and Corn, for celebrating the sounds, for reaffirmation of rhythm, for "Back in Memphis." Shout to the Africentric 80s and the PE power play.

Thanks to my powerful group of sister writers: Bridgett

Davis, Danzy Senna, and Amanda Inshall. Thank you, Sadie Lou sisters: Nikki, Erica, Aisha, Camille, and Rachel. Thank you, Sherron. Thank you, Erin and Val. Thank you, Zuhairah. Thank you, Tara, for the big dreams and for being *Fierce*.

Thank you, Chisholm fam: Grandmom, the matriarch, the Philly fashionista, and Shel She, Jimmy (who always was a performer), Tisa, Timmy (the band-man), Tony, and Terry. Thank you, Uncle Carlton. Thanks to the kids, especially Tony, Ibrahim, and Mahdiyyah. Thank you, Duguids: Grandmom, for keeping it all together, and Granddaddy, Erica, and Brett. Thanks to the kids, especially Courtney and Tre, Chanel, Marcus, and Paris, and Sydney-girl. And Ulens: Thank you, Uncle Lance, for your art. Thank you, Pop Pop, for writing, and for writing to me. Eternal presence. Thank you, Grandmom, may you rest in peace. Thank you, Mommy and Daddy, for the sweet memories of solidarity in the struggle. Thank you so much, Jim Stockton. All the aunties, uncles, and cousins—thank you. Thanks to the Bermuda family, all of you Astwoods, especially Aunt Belle and Aunt Jan for a home on the rock. Thank you to my in-laws, the Jones family and the Richardson family.

Thank you, Aunt Diane, for holding it all down on Frazier Street. And for smiling. And for your dance.

My husband. My source of power and strength. My deepest love. Thank you for being my life partner. *Habibi*.

Crystelle
Mourning

Eisa Nefertari Ulen

A Readers Club Guide

SUMMARY

Crystelle has a seemingly great life and a bright future. She lives in gentrified Brooklyn with a well-employed fiancé who wants to make her his wife, and she suspects she might be pregnant. The prospect of becoming a mother and wife, however, along with her recurring dreams of her murdered childhood sweetheart, send her emotions over the edge, and she heads back to her old inner-city Philadelphia neighborhood to face her past.

A CONVERSATION WITH EISA NEFERTARI ULEN

Crystelle's ties to her family, friends, and memories on Frazier Street are incredibly strong. Do you have similar feelings about the place where you grew up? Where is your Frazier Street?

Frazier Street is an actual place, not just a setting in my imagination. I was born in Philadelphia, where my mother and many family members grew up and still live. During my early childhood, until I turned ten years old, I lived in Harrisburg, Pennsylvania, which is where my father was raised and my paternal family members still live. The two cities are geographically close, and my parents and I would drive from Harrisburg to Philadelphia about once a month when I was young. We would stay at my maternal grandmother's house in the Mount

Airy section of Philly. I always visited my cousins, though. During summer vacations, my mother would send me to their house, in West Philadelphia, on Frazier Street. I'd stay there for weeks. Though my Aunt Diane passed away some years ago, I dedicated *Crystelle Mourning* to her because her home became the place I saw my female protagonist occupying as I began writing the novel.

The book is not autobiographical, though. None of the events in the novel, to my knowledge, have ever taken place on Frazier Street. While the book is a work of fiction, for me, psychically, Frazier Street exists in all our communities. To me, Frazier Street symbolizes home—not just home for Crystelle, but home for all African Americans. I tried to capture our communities in all their diverse complexity—the love and the violence, the close network of longtime neighbors and the isolation of one homeless woman, the folk struggling financially and the home owners with substantial savings. I tried to capture it all, the ugliness and the beauty, the weakness and the power of home.

Ghosts and spirits play such an important role in *Crystelle Mourning*. Do you believe in them?

I do. I believe the ancestors are with us. I believe the long-ago old souls can make themselves real in this world. I believe the babies waiting to be born can be active spirits, too, can nudge their parents and encourage them to embrace and bring them into this world. I believe in spirit.

I also believe in the ghosts of the past. I know that memories can haunt us. I think that so much of what haunts us are family ghosts. I'm thinking of the stories that are only whispered—or are never told at all. Crystelle is haunted by Jimmie, an actual spirit, but she is also haunted by the abortion. In some ways, Granddaddy is haunted by his joblessness in the North and the loss of the old family farm in the South. Mamma is haunted by the memory of her husband and his abandonment.

Music and dance are often included in your narrative. Do you have a background or any particular involvement in either?

I love to dance. Music is so important to me. I don't have a lot of formal training beyond a few ballet classes and flute and clarinet lessons as a girl, but I feel music deep, deep, deep in my bones.

You've included several poems within the story. How different is your process when writing poetry versus prose? Do you enjoy one style of writing over the other?

I don't think the process is much different. I write my creative work in the morning. I start as early as I possibly can. I have to write longhand, and I need to be able to gaze out my Brooklyn apartment window as I write. I enjoy writing both poetry and prose.

Should the reader assume that Crystelle is no longer mourning when the novel concludes?

I think the reader should let the work speak to them on a very personal level. Every interpretation of the work will be slightly different. For me, Crystelle is free of the ghosts that have been haunting her since Jimmie's murder and her abortion of their baby. My original thought was that Crystelle would stay locked in her madness, unable to let go of the ghosts of the past. That's not what the character wanted, though. During the writing process, she let me know she wanted to be free, so I released her. But the reader might feel some ambiguity with the ending, and that's okay with me.

Crystelle Mourning **largely portrays issues relating to the African American cultural experience. What are the experiences and themes in the novel that transcend race?**

Well, I hope all the major themes of the novel transcend race. As much as this book examines a particular experience regarding loss and recovery, and as much as the work is centered in the context of the African American experience, I think all people, cross-culturally, experience psychic trauma of some kind and must work toward recovery.

Violent death is, unfortunately, something that happens everywhere in the world, and all cultures have some history of violence and suffering on a massive scale. While the African American experience of forced displacement, slavery, and social violence is very specific, there are too many wars in this world, too many acts of genocide, too much loss, unfortunately, to think that the major themes of *Crystelle Mourning* would not transcend race. We, all of us around the world, have much more in common in terms of human experience than the superficial things, like race, that make us different.

You have published several pieces in various magazines and newspapers on social and cultural issues. Do you believe fictional writing can make the same social and cultural impact on readers as nonfiction?

I think maybe more. Fiction—art—is so provocative, so powerful, so empowering . . . I think both forms are important to those of us who think critically about culture and society. However, while you can read reports from the government and articles in newspapers and magazines about violence in the Black community, I hope that *Crystelle Mourning* does the important work of describing the impact of those statistical realities on Black people's personal lives. How do we make sense of senseless violence, of Black-on-Black crime, of the proliferation of guns in our neighborhoods? How do we celebrate our triumph over these difficult realities? I think art helps us do that.

In addition to being a published author, you're also an English professor. If your students were to remember only one lesson from your class, what would you want it to be?

Memory and Voice: Remember the Act and Tell It. My students, who come from all over the world, have seen so very much. I want them to bear witness to their personal truths.

Your uncle was the first Black elected Bermudian premier. Do you have strong ties to the island? What's your favorite activity when you visit?

I visit Bermuda every year, usually during Cup Match weekend, the holiday celebrating Emancipation on the island. My great-grandmother had fifteen brothers and sisters, but the descendants of those sixteen Bermudian siblings remain very close, I think. The first thing to do, after renting mopeds, is to zip around the tiny island with my husband and visit some of the elders. I try to see all my aunties during each visit. The next important thing, of course, is to head to the beach, dive in, and swim.

This was your first novel, though you have many other writing credits to your name. What literary projects are you working on now?

I'm working on my second novel. It's very exciting for me. This second work explores an African American family through the generations, from the capture of the family's African forefather in the early 1800s, through the family line, to one of his male descendants in the early 1980s. I was haunted by the image of a young man, captured, in chains, gazing up from the bottom of a slave ship as the wooden door locks him in, juxtaposed with his descendant, a young man, captured, in handcuffs, gazing out of a prison cell as the iron bars lock him in. These are the characters that want me to tell their stories now.

QUESTIONS AND TOPICS FOR DISCUSSION

1. The prologue has a second-person narrator, yet the rest of the book has a third-person omniscient narrator. Why does the author employ a different point of view in the opening pages? Did this affect your involvement in the story?

2. Dreams dominate this story, and a ghost plays a major role. What literary techniques are used to differentiate between dream states and reality, living characters and Jimmie's ghost? Why is Crystelle's spirit such an overwhelming aspect of her characterization?

3. The following appears on page 11: "'Remember this,' her disconnected self said out loud in her head. 'Life feasts on death.'" What does Crystelle mean by this? Would she say this at the end of the novel?

4. On page 53, Crystelle talks about the moths bumping into the light. Who do you think, besides the moths, Crystelle is referring to when she theorizes about why it happens?

5. How do you interpret the actions and dialogue of the homeless woman ("the crazy disco lady," page 96) in chapter four? Has the author included this character for symbolic or allegorical purposes?

6. What are Crystelle's true feelings for Hamp? Does she love him or is he simply a distraction from memories of Jimmie? Do their different backgrounds affect their relationship?

7. When Shelley became pregnant during college, her boyfriend stood by her and accepted his duties as the father. Consider the male characters—even those that are briefly mentioned—in this novel. On the whole, are men portrayed as reliable figures?

8. A shocking secret is exposed when Crystelle, Granddaddy, and Aunt Brenda discover Opal's role in Crystelle's abortion. How surprised were you to learn about this event subsequent to Jimmie's murder? Are Opal's actions forgivable?

9. What was your reaction to the poems, songs, and dialogue included before the prologue and at the beginning of several chapters (pages 126, 148, 162)? What function do they serve in relation to each subsequent chapter and the story as a whole?

10. Is there any irony in Crystelle's nickname, "Crystelle Clear"? By the conclusion of the novel, is Crystelle "clear"?

11. Among family, friends, and lovers, Crystelle has many significant relationships—and in a way, these relationships drive the plot of the book. Who do you think she relies upon the most and for what? Discuss Crystelle's relationships with the following characters and what emotional impact each has on her: Granddaddy, Opal, Aunt Brenda, Jimmie, Hamp, and Shelley.

ENHANCE YOUR BOOK CLUB

1. Poetry appears in several places throughout *Crystelle Mourning*. Have each member of your book club write his or her own poem to share. Try to mimic Eisa Ulen's poetic style.

2. Crystelle's time spent with her mother and granddaddy or Aunt Brenda often involves sharing a home-cooked meal. Before your book club meeting, ask each member to prepare a dish for a potluck dinner and enjoy the meal as you discuss *Crystelle Mourning*. Make sure it's Philadelphia-related! You can find some recipes for Philadelphia cheesecake at www.cooks.com/rec/search?q=philadelphia+cheesecake.

3. Crystelle helps Jimmie's mother sort through and throw away his old things and, in the process, they begin to heal. While this may be an especially emotional and difficult task, sifting through his everyday possessions also reminds them of a happiness once shared. In that positive spirit of sorting through the past, find something old of yours or something that belonged to a loved one that recalls a fond memory. Bring the item to your book club meeting and share your memory with the group.